The Young Rebels

'An informative and thought provoking read,
bringing 1916 alive for a new generation of children.'
The Irish Independent

Growing up in Texas, Morgan had two obsessions – horses and Ireland, the land of her grandparents. Before becoming a writer she worked with horses and was shortlisted for the USA Olympic dressage team in 1975, missing the final selection by just half of a percentage point. Then she took up writing. Her second novel, *Lion of Ireland*, dealt with the life of Ireland's greatest hero, Brian Boru. This book turned out to be a bestseller and was sold around the world in twenty-seven different countries.

Since then, Morgan has never looked back. She now lives in Ireland and her historical fiction titles continue to sell all over the globe. They include *Bard*, *Grania*, *On Raven's Wing* (titled *Red Branch* in the USA) and *Druids*.

Morgan has won numerous prestigious awards, including: Best Novel of the Year (USA, National League of Penwomen); Best Novel for Young Readers (American Library Association): National Historical Society Award (USA).

Her first two books for young readers, *Brian Boru* and *Strongbow*, won Bisto Book of the Year Awards in 1991 and 1992. Her other books include *Pirate Queen*, the story of Granuaile, *Star Dancer* and *Cave of Secrets*.

The YOUNG REBELS

Morgan Llywelyn

THE O'BRIEN PRESS
DUBLIN

First published 2006 by The O'Brien Press Ltd,
12 Terenure Road East, Rathgar, Dublin 6, D06 HD27, Ireland.
Tel: +353 1 4923333; Fax: +353 1 4922777
E-mail: books@obrien.ie
Website: www.obrien.ie
Reprinted 2007, 2012, 2013, 2015.

ISBN: 978-0-86278-579-6

Text © copyright Morgan Llywelyn 2006
Copyright for typesetting, design and editing
© The O'Brien Press Ltd

5 7 8 6
15 17 18 16

Cover photographs: Courtesy of Kilmainham Gaol
Printed and bound by CPI Group (UK) Ltd, Croydon, CR0 4YY
The paper used in this book is produced using pulp from managed forests

The O'Brien Press receives assistance from

For the boys of Killaloe National School

Contents

CHAPTER ONE

SEPTEMBER 1913

The rain taps the windowpane with cold, thin fingers as if it wants to get in.

I tap my desk with my own cold fingers because I want to get out. I don't like school and I don't like teachers. I want to climb trees and go fishing and never sit indoors in another classroom as long as I live.

Most of all, I want to see my mother. She's the most wonderful person in the whole world. I never say that out loud because the other boys would tease me, but it's true.

No matter how bold I've been Mam always understands that I meant no harm. She never loses her temper the way my father does. I can go to her with any problem.

Could go to her with any problem. But not any more.

The rain's falling harder now. Autumn is the worst time of the year. It's cold and grey and everything's dying.

My mother is very ill. When I go up to her room they tell me I'm in the way. I keep going back, though; I can't help it. It's like I can hear her calling to me, even though she hardly makes a sound these days.

My father's talking about sending me to the Christian Brothers. I overheard him say to Aunt Nell, 'I don't understand John Joe at all. I simply cannot cure the boy of acting out. Let the Brothers put manners on him like they did me.'

If my father caught me eavesdropping he would punish me severely. He punishes me a lot. Sometimes I don't even know what I've done wrong.

Mam hates it when he takes me out into the yard to cane me. I've seen her peer down from the upstairs window and beat her poor pale hands against the glass. Now she's too weak to get out of bed. I can remember when she was strong. When I was little and had night-mares Mam would hold me so tight that I knew nothing could hurt me ever.

My mother's widowed sister Nell has been stop-ping with us since Mam fell ill. She has her own little cottage in County Kildare and I wish she'd go back there. Aunt Nell smells like pickles and looks down her long thin nose at everyone except Mam. She only puts up with me for my mother's sake. She's well able for my father, though. Sometimes she takes my side just to annoy him.

'Beating won't improve John Joe,' I heard her say to him. 'The boy's rebellious enough already, that's why he was expelled from the National School.'

I'm not rebellious, I just hate being treated like a baby when I'm twelve years old. Well, almost twelve. I can read far above my age, but the adults don't give me credit for any brains at all. They should answer my questions and tell me how my mother really is. Week after week she gets paler and thinner. I'm awfully worried, but there's no one I can talk to about it.

Since Mam's been confined to her room my father's been beating me more than ever. Not because I've been bold, but just because I'm there.

Sending me to this school was Aunt Nell's idea. 'It will be perfect for John Joe,' she said. 'The fees are reasonable, and the courses include a thorough education in the classics. The pupils are kept busy from dawn until dark so there's no time to get into mischief.'

I didn't like the sound of that.

My father started to tell Aunt Nell to mind her own business, then changed his mind. They row a lot but he never goes too far. He's afraid Aunt Nell might leave. Then he would have to hire someone to care for Mam. He wouldn't like that. My father's always complaining about how much things cost – though he seems able to find plenty of money for drink.

Anyway he had Aunt Nell pack my things in a suitcase, and sent me here in a taxicab. I'm to be a boarder, trapped in this place day and night. I'm even forbidden to return home on the weekends though it's an easy bicycle ride. My father would not let me bring my bicycle.

Before the taxicab came for me, I ran up to Mam's room to tell her goodbye. She looked so small and frail in her bed. When she put up her poor thin arms to hug me there was no strength left in them. 'Be a good boy, John Joe,' she whispered against my cheek. Her breath was so warm on my skin it brought a lump to my throat.

Mam hardly ever speaks above a whisper any more, except when the doctor comes to the house. He makes her cry out. Once I ran into her room and hit him, and they had to pull me off him. If they would let me stay with Mam no one would ever hurt her again. I would protect her, so I would, like she used to protect me.

Instead I'm stuck in this dreadful place.

The Headmaster is watching me. He's a big, solid-built man, who wears a professor's black gown over his street clothes so he looks very solemn and dignified. I suppose he could be called handsome except for a slight squint in one eye.

This is only my second day here but I hate him already.

'John Joe, do I have your attention?' the Head asks. The other boys turn around in their seats to look at me. I hate them too.

'Yes sir.'

He walks along between the desks and stops by mine. When he looks down at me I lift my chin and glare back, to show I'm not afraid of him.

Then something funny happens. He seems to see right inside me. Can he tell that I'm afraid after all? 'I know this is difficult for you, lad,' the Head says in a gentle voice, 'but you're among friends here.'

I don't want his sympathy. I just want to go home.

The boy whose bed is to the right of mine in the dormitory is called Roger. He's a stocky lad who gives himself airs because his father's a bank manager. The boy on my left is the son of a man who stokes the furnace in one of the big hotels. Yet we're all treated alike. We sleep on identical narrow iron beds and take our meals together in the refectory. The same meals for everyone.

There are no special treats for boys who can pay extra.

When I first saw St Enda's I was astonished. I never imagined ordinary Irish boys could have a school like this. It's an eighteenth-century house built in the Georgian style; a small mansion really, three storeys high, with classical columns across the front. When the sun shines on the granite walls they look almost golden. The house was built as a country retreat for the gentry, and was named the Hermitage. One can imagine wealthy men in tall hats and pretty ladies in white dresses playing croquet on the lawn.

Now the sign on the wrought iron gates at the foot of the drive reads 'Scoil Éanna'– Saint Enda's School. There is a playing field for sports instead of croquet. In fact, or so Aunt Nell told me, everything about the school has been planned with the health and happiness of the students in mind.

I don't believe her. What sort of school does that?

The interior of the Hermitage is surprisingly plain, almost underfurnished. There aren't any rugs except in the drawing room, and footsteps echo on the stairs. I get the feeling that the Pearses don't have much money to spend on luxuries. But everything is neat and clean. All the woodwork is polished to a deep, rich glow. One can smell the beeswax that's used on the furniture, and the lavender that's sprinkled on the bed linen.

Someone spends a lot of love and care on this house.

Mam used to spend love and care on our house, which is not nearly so grand as this one. Just a red-brick terraced house with a broken iron railing in front. The bricks are blackened with coal dust.

I want to go home.

The Hermitage stands in its own parkland, comprising fifty acres near the village of Rathfarnham. From the great tall windows, one can see the nearby Dublin mountains. There are spectacular views in every direction. The lawns around the house are dotted with trees and shrubs and flower borders. There is also an orchard, plus a poultry yard and a walled vegetable garden convenient to the kitchen at the rear of the house.

Fifty acres is a lot of land, especially to a city lad like me. On my first full day at St Enda's, the boy called Roger was assigned to show me around the grounds. Roger had a bag of sweets in his pocket and ate them one after another, but he didn't offer any to me. He even walked in front of me so I couldn't see how many he was eating.

I could see how broad his backside was, though. From behind he looked like our coal man's horse. Watching him plod along in front of me gave me the first smile I've had in a long time.

After a short walk, the smooth lawns around the Hermitage gave way to a woodland alive with songbirds. Inviting paths meandered off in every direction. 'Stay behind me or you'll get lost,' Roger said, as if I was too stupid to find my own way. I ignored him. I told myself, 'I don't take orders from horses who pull coal wagons.' Then I smiled again.

The woods were amazing. I never saw so many trees perfect for climbing! There was even a miniature mountain glen with a rushing stream at the bottom, and a deep, cold pool. Roger told me the boys were allowed to swim there. He also showed me a little stone building called 'Emmet's Fort', that could be almost anything. 'We like to play pirates here,' he said.

I would enjoy playing pirates, if I felt like playing at all.

St Enda's is very much a family affair. The Headmaster, his widowed mother, his two sisters, and his brother, live here at the school. Their rooms are up at the top of the house. The women take care of the housekeeping and everyone teaches classes as well, except for the Head's mother. She's the cook. I have to say, the food here is better than I get at home. My aunt only knows how to cook bacon and cabbage, beans on toast, or boiled mutton. Full stop. Yesterday at St Enda's we were served the most gorgeous roast chicken and stuffing, seasoned with herbs from the walled garden. I said I wasn't hungry – I didn't think I was – but before I knew it, I'd cleaned my plate.

The students raise most of the fruit and vegetables we eat, and the eggs and chickens too. It's actually part of our course of study. I never heard of such a thing before.

One of my new classmates claims, 'Vegetables taste better when you've grown them yourself.'

He may think so but I never shall. I hate vegetables. Brussels sprouts, ugh!

Roger complains because there is no heat in the dormitory. He's a Protestant boy, one of the first I've ever met. There are several here, however. Roger's family has a big detached house in Rathgar. He keeps a sepia photograph of it on the windowsill nearest his bed and keeps whinging about how uncomfortable St Enda's is by comparison. 'At home we have a fireplace in every room,' he claims.

I doubt it. I never heard of anyone who had a fireplace in every room.

The Headmaster's brother tells Roger, 'Sleeping in a cold room is better for you. At St Enda's we hope to build healthy bodies as well as good minds.'

I hate the Headmaster. He's a cold, aloof man, like headmasters everywhere. The sudden appearance of

17

the Head, or even the sound of his footstep in the corridor, is enough to put an end to the roughest horseplay.

I want to hate his brother, too, but it's hard to hate Willie. He likes us to call him Willie, there's nothing pompous or aloof about him. He's a dark, slender man with a shy smile. Willie teaches art at St Enda's and Margaret, the Head's older sister, teaches French. Willie also coaches handball in a court behind the main building. We're encouraged to take part in a wide variety of sports, but if there's something we really don't enjoy we don't have to do it.

'Sport teaches discipline,' the Headmaster says. 'You are allowed a high degree of personal freedom at St Enda's, but remember: true freedom can exist only where there is self discipline.'

St Enda's is unlike any other school in Ireland. It offers lots of subjects that have never been available to Irish children, except perhaps the very few whose parents can afford to send them to England for an education. Here boys are prepared to become 'complete men' – whatever that means. We study art and drama and music as well as scholarly subjects. A lot of time is spent on sports to make us strong and healthy, and we learn practical things like building and plumbing and how to sew and mend our clothes. Also, St Enda's is bilingual. The Head went to Belgium to study the way bilingual schools there are organised. Most of our studies, except for French and Latin, are taught through the Irish.

I hate the Irish language, it's the language of poverty. Unfortunately it's one thing we have no choice about.

I wonder if my father realised this is a bilingual school? If he knew he might not make me stay here. He shares the government's contempt for everything Irish. The attitude is: everything that's English or from England is noble and fine. Anything that's Irish – meaning native to this country – is dirty and stupid.

Why would anyone go to all the trouble to create a school like St Enda's for boys who are dirty and stupid?

My first weekend at St Enda's will be hard. I know I'll feel lonelier than ever. The day pupils will go home and only a few of us will be left here. There used to be more boarders but some of them have dropped out. The Head and the other teachers support a political movement which is not popular with everyone. Irish nationalism.

I don't see why a school should be involved in politics. Politics is as boring as history, which I hate. Neither has anything to do with me. While my classmates and I are on our way to the refectory, I say in a rather loud voice, 'Studying things that happened donkey's years ago is as stupid as studying a language nobody uses anymore.'

We return from our collation to find the Head in our classroom, writing on the blackboard. He puts down the chalk, gives me a long look, and leaves the room. On the blackboard is written, 'The Irish language is your special birthright. It is a secret code that belongs only to you.'

I never had a secret code before.

To my surprise, I have learned that the students do most of the maintenance at St Enda's. That includes caring for the grounds. I wonder what Aunt Nell would say if she knew her nephew had become a common labourer. I'll bet Roger doesn't do any gardening in Rathgar.

My first Saturday at the school is fine and dry, so we are put to digging flower beds under the supervision of Michael MacRory, the gardener here. Mr MacRory has a baldy head. Some of the boys slag him about it, but he just laughs and says, 'Sure grass never grew on a busy street.'

I am quietly pleased to see that Mr MacRory gives Roger a big shovel and assigns him to do some heavy digging. Roger mutters a lot under his breath until Mr MacRory says, 'Speak up lad, share the joke with all of us!' Roger turns bright red and digs silently.

When we finish the flower beds we set out new shrubs and rake the pathways. Other schools would hire a whole crew of men for such work, but here the students take care of everything ourselves. We even collect and burn the rubbish.

I never planted a bush before. When I turn over the soil with my spade the earth smells sweet.

On Sunday I go to Mass with the other Catholic boarders. In the afternoon we gather on the lawn. The sun is out and the house glimmers like gold in its green setting. The fragrance of fairy cakes baking in the kitchen drifts across out to us. I suppose St Enda's isn't so bad. In fact it's really quite beautiful.

It's peaceful here, too. I believe the word is 'serene'. One has a sense of being far away from everything that is ugly or troubling.

Serene was one of Mam's favourite words.

As we sit in a circle on the grass, one of our teachers, Mr MacDonagh, who writes poems and lectures at university, reads Irish poetry aloud to us. His full name is Thomas MacDonagh and he helped Mr Pearse found this school. Mr MacDonagh reads slowly, pronouncing the words clearly so we don't miss any. He is a cheerful, friendly little man who tells funny stories, some of them in Irish. Even if I don't understand the language I can understand his expressions and gestures.

I'm surprised by the rhythm of the old language. It sounds almost like singing, the way Mam used to sing around the house before she fell ill. When the other boys laugh, I ask to know the joke too. Thomas repeats the Irish, gives the English translation, then recites in Irish again.

'Now,' he says, 'who can repeat that last line in English?' Most of the boys put up their hands and he selects one. I could have done it myself if I wanted to.

Then he asks, 'Who can say the last line in Irish?'

I still don't put up my hand, but I think I could do that too. I might not be able to pronounce every word correctly, but I could come close. I know I could. It's a witty poem about a wicked king and a brave poet who put him to shame. If I memorise the entire poem for Mam, maybe I can make her laugh.

If – I mean when – she gets stronger, I should like to bring her out here. Maybe the Pearses would give her a room with windows looking toward the mountains. In such a serene setting, I just know she would get well.

When the lilacs bloom I could bring her armloads of blossom for her room. Lilac is her favourite scent.

CHAPTER TWO

OCTOBER 1913

The Headmaster of St Enda's takes in strays.

In August there was a lockout in the city as the result of a labour union strike, and a riot resulted. Several of the workers were killed by the police. Their leader, a man called Larkin, was arrested. The government ordered the schools to refuse admittance to his children, but our Head ignored the order. One of the Larkin boys is in my dormitory. I wonder how he felt about his father's arrest. That's almost as bad as having a sick mother, I guess.

After a few weeks Mr Larkin was released on bail. His son says he's gone to England to raise funds for the men who are locked out. While he's away a man called

James Connolly is taking over as leader of the workers. None of his boys is in school here, though. Roger says that's just as well, because there are enough 'working class' boys at St Enda's already.

The Head doesn't like us to talk about someone's 'class'. I don't know why. Other people discuss it all the time.

He really does take in strays. All sorts of injured creatures find their way here, and we boys are expected to take care of them. 'The only boy ever expelled from this school was made to leave because he hurt a cat,' one of my classmates tells me.

I've never had a pet. My father doesn't want the mess and trouble of animals in the house.

The Head's brother shows us how to splint a bird's broken leg using a drinking straw. 'Remember that this little bird is one of God's creations just as you are,' he says.

I stare down at the little bird, who is opening and closing its beak very rapidly. I never thought of an animal as a living creation of God before.

Caring for the bird with the broken leg falls to me. I'm delighted with myself when it begins to get well. Maybe I can be a doctor someday. If I am, I'll never cause pain to anyone.

There is a telephone in the Headmaster's office. One

must ask permission to use it. I apply to the Head's mother, a plump, grey-haired lady with a soft voice and a sweet smile. 'My Mam is quite ill and I want to ring home,' I explain.

'Bless you, lad, of course you do. And so you shall.' Before she escorts me to the Headmaster's office she gives me a quick hug. I'm not used to being hugged and don't know how to react. She smells of soap and lavender water.

The Headmaster is seated behind his desk, writing in a large book. He stands up when his mother enters the room. She explains the situation, then leaves us alone together. I wish she would stay but don't dare ask, it would make me sound like a baby.

'Do you know how to use a telephone, John Joe?' the Head inquires.

'I do not know how, sir.'

'Here, I'll show you.'

Then the Head leaves me alone in his office so I can have privacy. This will be the first time I've ever placed a telephone call. The telephone is not a toy. Children are not permitted to use one. Even big boys who smoke store-bought cigarettes and ride their bicycles into the centre of Dublin have never used a telephone.

I feel quite grown up, making a telephone call in the Headmaster's office.

Facing the front windows is a big desk piled high with papers. The desk is surrounded on three sides by bookcases overflowing with books. More books are stacked on the floor. The whole room smells of them, a paper-and-leather smell. It's very quiet in here, too, with a great feeling of ... peace, I guess. Peace is as soft as dust, as comforting as cushions.

After I ask the telephone operator to connect me, I have to wait a long time until Aunt Nell comes on the line. The first thing she says is 'What's wrong?' in her sharp voice. She often begins conversations with those words, as if something must always be wrong.

'I want to know how Mam is.'

'She's in good form,' my aunt replies, but she says it too quickly. I know she's lying. They must think I'm stupid. The Head doesn't think I'm stupid, he trusts me to use the telephone by myself.

'If she's in good form, may I come home?'

'You'll stay right where you are, John Joe. The fee has been paid and that's all there is to it.'

'Please, Aunt Nell, can't I at least–' The instrument goes click. Then it makes a sound like a fingernail on a blackboard.

I stand holding the receiver in my hand. I want to scream at it.

Instead I begin grabbing up the papers on the desk

and throwing them around the room. Some I wad into balls and hurl at the windows. When I have papers all over the floor I begin with the books.

I don't even notice the Headmaster enter the room until he's standing right beside me. I freeze. He's going to do what any teacher would do, march me outside and beat the living tar out of me with an ash plant. He can never make me cry, though. My father taught me that. If I cried, my father kept on hitting me until I stopped. 'That's how to make a man of you,' he claimed.

I double my fists and glare up at the Head.

'When you are finished here, John Joe, and have it all out of your system,' he says calmly, 'please gather up the papers and books and put them where you found them.'

Then he turns and walks out of the room. Leaving me alone.

I don't understand this man.

The Head has taken our class himself this morning. He is talking of the future and how to prepare ourselves for it. 'Some of you boys might consider teaching as a profession,' he tells us. 'It is among the highest of callings. A teacher takes a grave responsibility upon himself: the moulding of the most sensitive of all God's creations: a human mind.

'It is essential that the teacher understand the world of his pupils. For example, a teacher in the Infant School should show a keen interest in the puppies and kittens the children have at home. In Primary School the teacher of boys should be thoroughly aware of the rules for marbles and leap-frog, while a teacher of girls should know how to skip rope and care for dolls. A Secondary School teacher needs to be comfortable with hurling and football, or baking and dressmaking.'

I never heard of a teacher taking any interest in the things that interested his pupils before. Maybe I could be a teacher someday.

My father would hate that. He doesn't think teachers make enough money, which is true, I suppose. Most of those who teach here work at other jobs as well. The Head does a lot of writing and editing for magazines and periodicals.

It's hard to explain about the Headmaster of St Enda's. Boys tend to think of teachers as the enemy because they prevent us from doing things we want to do. When the father of one of the day pupils came out to the school yesterday, I happened to overhear a conversation between him and the Head as they stood in the front passage. 'My son has no interest in books or study,' the man was complaining. 'All he wants to do is make the most appalling noise on an old tin-whistle he found somewhere. What am I to do with the little good-for-nothing?'

'The answer is obvious,' the Head replied quite seriously. 'Buy him a good tin-whistle.'

Without asking permission, another boy has taken several old wooden shutters and built himself a sort of hideaway out in the woods. When the Head finds out about it he sends Willie into the city to purchase some timber and sheets of tin. 'Every man should know how to build a house for himself,' says the Head.

We boys are put to work sawing the timber into little planks and cutting tiny nails and door hinges from the tin. Then we are shown how to draw up plans for building houses. By spring, each of us will have completed an entire miniature house, including making bits of furniture. I never thought I could do such a thing, but I can. We all can.

The Headmaster is not our enemy.

Today we're writing compositions. When I turn mine in, the teacher comments, 'You could improve this by being a bit more lyrical.'

When I ask Mr MacDonagh for a definition of lyrical, he replies with a smile, 'Lyrical is what makes your heart sing'.

The only thing I can think of that makes my heart sing is hot porridge on a cold morning. Does that mean porridge is lyrical?

I'm also studying Latin and maths and literature, but my favourite class is History because it's full of battles and great deeds. Not English history, which is all I was taught in National School, but Irish history. The history of Ireland goes back thousands of years, long before there was any writing. History was passed down from generation to generation by the druids, who memorised everything. The Head says that each time a history book is written changes are made, but when something is memorised – it took the druids as much as twenty years of study – it is carved on the mind and almost impossible to change.

We boys can speak English outside of class, but when one of our teachers praises us – which they often do, surprisingly – it's always in Irish. It's amazing how quickly one can learn a language in order to hear good things about oneself.

Mr MacDonagh instructs us in what he calls 'our native tongue'. He says we're all part of one family, the Irish family. Even Roger, I suppose, though it's hard to think of Roger as a brother. It's a funny thing about Roger, though. He's very good at maths; he can calculate huge sums in his head. When I have trouble with multiplication he shows me an easy shortcut.

I guess I can't call him names in my head any more.

One day Mr MacDonagh brings a photo album to the school to show us pictures of his pretty wife and young children. He's very proud of his children, and tells us delightful stories about them.

I wonder if my father is proud of me? He certainly never shows it. Everything I do is wrong, according to him.

I'm convinced that Thomas MacDonagh has eyes in the back of his head, hidden in his curly hair. He can be standing at the blackboard with his back turned to the class and suddenly say, 'Do not pick your nose, John Joe.'

How can he tell?

To his credit, he doesn't go banging on about it. One correction should be enough; that's the policy at St Enda's. It's funny how well it works.

Mr MacDonagh has a mischievous side, too. He enjoys playing pranks as much as we do. The Head is too dignified for pranks, yet I've heard him laugh out loud at the jokes Mr MacDonagh tells.

The Head has a wonderful laugh, a deep warm rumble that comes right up from his belly. It makes one feel good just to hear it.

In Irish the word for Headmaster is *Ardmháistir*.

The Ardmháistir has a friend called Constance, Countess Markievicz, who is the wife of a Polish noble-man. She herself is Irish. Well, Anglo-Irish. Upper Class, the Ascendancy and all of that. Her family has estates in Sligo, but she doesn't live the life I imagine other wealthy women do. She's very involved with the labour movement. Together with a man called Bulmer Hobson, four years ago she founded an Irish boy scout troop. She named it Na Fianna Éireann, after the army of Fionn Mac Cumhaill. I didn't know who Fionn was until I came here, they never told us about him in the National School.

A company of the Fianna has been organised at St Enda's by a young apprentice teacher called Con Col-bert. Most of the students here belong to it. I've watched them drilling like real soldiers on the playing field and they look terribly serious, but one can tell they're having great fun.

I want to join the Fianna, but Con Colbert says I have to have permission from home first. I shall write the letter tonight.

Roger says he's going to write one too, and asks me how many 'esses' there are in the word 'permission'. Maybe he can do maths, but I can spell.

After several days I receive a reply to my letter. It's not from my father, though. Aunt Nell writes that my request is denied because my mother is afraid I might be hurt. Mam doesn't understand the kind of things boys like to do. She wants to keep me wrapped in cotton wool.

She's the one who needs to be wrapped in cotton wool.

My mother's not getting any better. The Ardmháistir lets me ring home whenever I want, but no one will tell me what's happening with her. I knew they wouldn't. They will have to let me come home for Christmas, though. Then I shall learn the truth.

Meanwhile I am learning other things. I was wrong about the Ardmháistir. He appears stuffy, but he isn't, not really. I think that's only the face he wears because it's expected of him. He takes his meals in the family dining room with his mother and sisters, but sometimes he joins us in the refectory afterward. He's not nearly so serious then. He leaves off his academic robe and sits with us in his shirtsleeves, as if he's just another boy. He knows wonderful stories about ancient heroes and can recite reams of poetry by heart. Once or twice he even joins us in a sing-song.

The Ardmháistir writes plays, too. We are going to put one on here later this month. Some of his plays have been produced in the Abbey Theatre, with boys from this school acting the parts. I would like to be in one of the plays but my Irish isn't good enough. I'm improving, though. Mr MacDonagh says I have an ear for languages.

My own family would never say such a thing to me. They're afraid I would get above my station.

The Ardmháistir says if Ireland was a republic we wouldn't have such things as 'class' and 'getting above your station'. In a republic all men, and all women too, are equal under the law.

Ireland is not a republic, but part of the British Empire, the huge area that's in pink on the map of the world. The Empire contains both slaves and masters. Still, is it not better to be a small part of something grand, like an empire, rather than a little republic all on its own, with no power and no glory? That's what my father says anyway. He's in the civil service, working for the government in Dublin Castle.

I don't want to become a civil servant. I don't want to be anything like my father.

Although the Ardmháistir rarely talks about himself, one can tell that he's proud of his parents. His late father was a Protestant, an Englishman who came to Dublin in his youth and never went back. He acquired no small measure of fame as a monumental sculptor, producing a number of fine statues and altars for Catholic churches. Eventually he became a

Catholic himself, like the Ardmháistir's mother.

Most of the boys at St Enda's are Catholics. But the Ardmháistir says religion must never be divisive – meaning it must never be used to divide people. Protestant students like Roger are welcome here. They can attend their own churches, but aside from that they receive the same education as the rest of us, with a strong emphasis on Christian prayer and moral standards.

'It is the same God for all of us,' the Ardmháistir says. 'We just speak to him in different ways.'

Jim Larkin's son is very downhearted. His father has been sentenced to seven months in prison. I don't think that's fair, the man was only trying to stand up for the workers who are badly exploited. Would Christ not have done the same thing?

This afternoon I used the telephone to ring home and ask about my mother. I got the same answer as always, which is no answer at all.

Tonight in the dormitory I pick a fight with Roger. 'I'm tired of your complaining,' I tell him. 'What do you have to complain about anyway? You don't know what troubles are.'

I'm a little taller, but Roger is heavier than me. However I've heard the Ardmháistir say that size doesn't matter.

I give Roger a bloody nose.

He goes crying to Mrs Pearse.

In the morning I am summoned to the Head's office. 'You want to be thrown out of this school,' states the Ardmháistir. It is not a question.

'No sir,' I lie. But I do want to be thrown out. I want to go home while there's still a chance to see Mam.

He looks at me across his desk. 'I despise bullies and bullying, John Joe. There will be none of either in this school. Do you understand?'

I put my fists on my hips and thrust out my lower lip. My father calls it my bold expression.

The Ardmháistir stands up with a sigh and comes toward me. 'Hold out your hands,' he says. I expect him to strike them with a ruler. I know what that's like, it's been done to me lots of times.

Instead he holds out his hands and takes both of mine. 'I'm afraid you do want to leave us,' he says gently. 'But sometimes what we want is the very worst thing we could get, John Joe. If you are expelled you will not be living up to your full potential. Is failure what you really want?'

'Failure?' I echo. It is a damp, sad word.

Although the Ardmháistir's face is full, almost fleshy, I am aware of unyielding bones beneath. 'Failure,' he says, 'means knuckling the forelock to people who think they are better than you.' Patrick Henry Pearse, who prefers to be called Padraic, speaks in a low, hard voice I never heard him use before.

CHAPTER THREE

NOVEMBER 1913

Margaret, the Ardmháistir's older sister, instructs us in French. She's a good teacher but takes no nonsense from us. The younger sister is called Mary Brigid, and she plays the harp. She's said to be 'temperamental'. I'm not quite sure what it means, but it's not good. When I was very little we had a brown pony and a dogcart with a red leather seat, and Mam took me for drives in the country. Mam's parents, who are dead now, had given her that pony and cart before she married.

But my father sold the pony because he said it was temperamental.

I don't think the Pearses can sell Mary Brigid, though

they might wish they could. She has 'turns' sometimes, when no one can control her. She laughs or cries for no reason and has to be sent to her room. Otherwise she would disrupt the entire school. Her brothers are very gentle with her. Neither of them loses his temper, no matter what she does.

I still lose my temper at Roger sometimes. Some people are just born to be irritating, I guess, like having a splinter under your fingernail. But he's not a bad sort, really.

Students at St Enda's have to take some outdoor exercise every day, no matter what the weather. The grounds are our own private park, with endless ways to amuse ourselves. I'm even learning how to swim in the pond. The Ardmháistir insists that every boy learn how to swim. He has a horror of drowning.

On weekends the Ardmháistir leads us on nature walks. He is enthralled by the beauty of Ireland's scenery and we are caught up in his enthusiasm. He often stops along the way to lecture on the flora and fauna. Mr MacDonagh claims, laughingly, that the Ardmháistir started the school in order to make as many speeches as he likes.

In addition to coaching us in handball, Willie referees boxing matches. I'm learning to box but sometimes I hit a little too hard. Willie says the same was true of his brother. 'Pat was an outstanding boxer in school, but he had a hot temper. Finally he stopped boxing altogether because he was afraid he might hurt someone.'

St Enda's competes against other schools in various sporting events and has won a number of awards. The favourite sport here is hurling, which the Ardmháistir calls 'The game of Cúchulainn'. I love hurling! I can play as hard as I like without worrying about Mam worrying about me, because she doesn't know.

Roger could be good at hurling but he hangs back. Maybe he's afraid of being hurt. Fear can make you sick in the pit of your stomach.

In the late afternoon, when the shadows lie long on the playing field, the Ardmháistir comes out to watch us. He only stays for a little while, then goes back in his office. He edits periodicals and writes poetry and carries on a huge correspondence. Much of his work involves raising more money for the school. His light burns late into the night and in the morning he often looks exhausted, though he's not an old man. I don't think he's much above thirty.

I don't hate the Ardmháistir any more. It's hard to hate a man who's practically killing himself for you.

Yesterday I learned that he founded not only our school but also a similar school for girls, called St Ita's.

Running two schools was terribly expensive, and he got no help from the government because his ideas are so different. Finally he had to close St Ita's. I'm glad he was able to keep St Enda's open. I wonder why he doesn't marry and have children of his own. Any child would be lucky to have Padraic Pearse for a father.

Perhaps he's just too busy. He's been going to a lot of important meetings in the city recently.

While collecting the rubbish from the kitchen I ask the Ardmháistir's mother – she is the sort of woman you feel you can ask anything – if he will marry someday. 'There was a girl once,' she says, with a faraway look in her eye. 'A lovely girl called Eveleen Nicholls. She and Pat had many things in common, they even shared the same political philosophy. Sadly, she was drowned.'

I am fascinated, I never knew anyone who drowned. 'What happened?' I ask eagerly.

'The Nicholls family was acquainted with Tomás Ó Criomhthain,' Mrs Pearse tells me, 'a native speaker who lived with his family on Great Blasket Island. Eveleen often went there on holiday to improve her knowledge of Irish. She once took Pat with her, in fact. Had he not fallen in love with Connemara he might have built a summer home on the Blaskets, but all that was spoilt for him when Eveleen died.' Mrs

Pearse takes a handkerchief out of her sleeve and dabs at her eyes.

I'm impatient for her to get on with the story. Why do adults take so long to get to the good part? I want to hear about the drowning. How did it happen? Who found her? What did the body look like afterward?

'During Eveleen's visits to the Blaskets she and Cáit Ó Criomhthain, one of Tomás' daughters, became close friends,' Mrs Pearse continues at last. 'One fine afternoon Eveleen and Cáit decided to go bathing at a strand below the cottage. They were accompanied by Cáit's younger brother Dónal, who was only fourteen.

'Perhaps the two girls went out too far, or a freak wave came in and caught them. They suddenly found themselves in trouble anyway. Poor Dónal tried to go to their rescue but was drowned in the attempt. As for Eveleen ... ' Mrs Pearse's voice breaks. The handkerchief appears again. 'Eveleen saved her friend Cáit at the cost of her own life.

'The circumstances of the drowning were widely reported in the national newspapers. The funeral was one of the largest ever held in Dún Chaoin, I believe. My Pat went down for it. His feelings run deep, too deep for his own good, perhaps. When Eveleen died I think his heart went into the grave with her, for he has not looked at a woman since. Instead he devotes himself to educating the children he will never have. You lads are his life now.'

In the library I've found a slim volume of poems written by the Ardmháistir. One is entitled 'I Have Not Garnered Gold':

I have not garnered gold;
The fame I found hath perished.
In love I got but grief
That withered my life.
Of riches or of store
I shall not leave behind me
(Yet I deem it, O God, sufficient)
But my name in the heart of a child.

Last night the Pearse brothers went into Dublin. My anxiety about Mam has kept me awake all night, so I hear them returning close to dawn. I don't know why I go out onto the landing, it is very cold. My feet are like two blocks of ice. When I sneeze the Ardmháistir hears me and comes running up the stairs.

'What are you doing out here, John Joe?' he asks as he takes off his coat and wraps it around me.

'I couldn't sleep.'

'Well, you must sleep now. I'm going to do the same, if only for a few hours. But this has been a night to celebrate. The twenty-fifth of November will go down in history.'

'Why is that, sir?'

'Do you know the meaning of Home Rule, John Joe?' Before I can say anything Mr Pearse answers his own question. 'If Britain granted Ireland Home Rule, this country would have a limited form of self-government. She is entitled to no less. For almost two thousand years Ireland was ruled by her own kings. This was a prosperous island, rich in timber and gold and cattle, until foreigners came to plunder and enslave. Our greatest High King, Brian Boru, defeated the Vikings in 1014, but within a hundred years our sovereignty had been taken from us by the kings of England. This proud land was driven to her knees.

'Yet she never forgot that once, she had been free.

'Since the last century Ireland has sought Home Rule. Britain has always refused. Now, when at last there is some support for our cause in Parliament, northern Protestants have formed a militia called the Ulster Volunteer Force. The UVF is sworn to prevent Home Rule by force, if necessary. Members of the British government are openly supplying them.'

'Supplying them with what, sir?'

'Guns, John Joe,' he says bluntly. 'Massive quantities of guns and armaments. My friends and I do not believe a small minority in the north has the right to deny a measure of freedom to this entire island. Nor do we like being threatened.

'Tonight I attended a meeting in the Rotunda, where an organization called the Irish National Volunteer Corps was founded to counter the UVF. For the first time the people of Ireland will have an armed force under *Irish* command to protect them.' His voice rings in the dark stairwell.

A shiver runs up my spine. But not because I am cold.

CHAPTER FOUR

DECEMBER 1913

Nine days after the founding of the Irish Volunteers the government issues a proclamation banning the import of arms and ammunition into Ireland. I wonder if there's a connection? Apparently the government does not mind the Ulster Volunteers bringing in guns. There's always been one law in this country for Protestants and another for Catholics.

Sometimes Roger acts like there's one law for him and another for the rest of us. But I notice, as time goes by, that he's getting better about it.

I'm going home for Christmas. Mrs Pearse comes to the dormitory to be certain I have everything packed. 'I've brought some fairy cakes for you to take home,' she tells me. They are wrapped in tissue paper and tied with tiny blue ribbons.

In art class we made Christmas cards for our families. I didn't know I could draw, but I've produced quite a decent angel with folded wings, bending over the manger where the Christ child lies. One of my classmates said it looks like the child in the painting that hangs in the front hall of the school. An Irish artist who is a great admirer of the Ardmháistir painted that picture. When I look at it I imagine it's a portrait of my little sister, the one who died when she was being born.

Mam has never been well since. Tonight I shall go to the chapel and pray for her.

There will be no Christmas for me. Not this year, maybe not ever. As I'm coming out of the chapel I meet the Ardmháistir, who has been looking for me. The expression on his face almost makes my heart stop. A great cold stone settles in my stomach, and I know the worst. He doesn't have to tell me.

The Ardmháistir himself is taking me home. Only a few weeks ago there was nothing I wanted so much. Now I do not want to go at all.

The house where my mother died. How can I walk through that door and up that stair? How can I enter the room where she is laid out waiting for me? It is too terrible.

Without my saying anything, Mr Pearse knows how I feel. He too has lost someone he loves. 'Do you want me to go in with you?' he asks.

'Yes. I mean no. Yes, please, sir,' I finally say.

He takes my hand and we walk up to the door together.

I do not remember the house ever being so cold. No fires are lit. Some black stuff is draped over the looking glass in the front passage, and the clock has been stopped. There are people in the parlour, neighbours, mostly, speaking in whispers. When we enter the room they glance in my direction and then look away again as if they are embarrassed.

I'm still holding tight to the Ardmháistir's hand.

When I was a little lad I held tight to Mam's hand when we went to the shops. I loved going to the shops with her. She always gave me a penny to spend on any sweets I liked.

So I always bought the ones I knew that she liked, too.

Who am I going to share my sweets with now?

Pain goes through me like a knife. My throat is all choked up with tears I'm trying not to shed. Oh, Mam. Oh, Mam!

Aunt Nell comes toward us. Her eyes are red with crying. It's all right for women to cry. 'Poor little lad,' she says. Not to me, but to the Ardmháistir. 'Is he ready to go up and kiss his mother goodbye?'

My stomach is colder than the house. My feet seem to have grown to the floor.

My father stands on the other side of the room with his pipe in his hand. He's not smoking, he's just holding it. On his face there is no absolutely no expression.

Aunt Nell beckons to him. 'Here's John Joe come to see his mother.'

Moving like a man whose joints have rusted, my father puts his pipe down on the mantelpiece. He will never come to me, I shall have to go to him. Tugging the Ardmháistir after me, I start across the room. Suddenly I drop Mr Pearse's hand and hurl myself against my father, throwing my arms around him in a desperate hug. I don't know what's come over me, I've never done anything like this before.

My father stands rigid in my embrace for a moment. Then he pushes me away. And slaps me.

There is a shocked gasp in the room.

Quicker than I thought he could move, the Ardmháistir steps between me and my father.

There is another shocked gasp in the room.

Mr Pearse says quietly, 'I realise this is a difficult time for you, sir, and you have my deepest sympathy, but I cannot condone your behaviour.'

My father's face starts to turn red. He's wearing an expression now, one I know all too well. 'I won't have the boy making a show of himself!' he exclaims angrily.

'The boy just lost his mother. He was coming to you for comfort.'

'I just lost my wife,' my father retorts, 'and I'll thank you to leave, sir. This is none of your business.' His face is getting redder.

Seeing them together I realise that the Ardmháistir is much larger than my father. My father is a little, angry man who does not know what to do with his anger. It sprays out of his mouth like spittle. Aunt Nell hurries over to us and puts one hand on her brother's arm. 'Please, Bertie. Not in front of the neighbours.' She throws a pleading glance at Mr Pearse.

The Ardmháistir inclines his head toward me. 'If you want to go upstairs, John Joe, I'll go with you.'

The next thing I know we are in Mam's room. One of her cousins is sitting by the bed. Mr Pearse says something to her and she leaves. I pay no attention; I can see nothing, feel nothing, think of nothing but my mother. She is so still. Her face is as white as the sheet tucked under her chin. Her hands are folded atop the covers with her rosary laced through her fingers. I stand by the bed, looking down at her. Time seems to have stopped.

I shall never see her again.

How can that be? This is a bad dream, it has to be. In a few minutes I shall wake up in my bed in St Enda's and ...

Slowly, I bend down until my lips almost touch Mam's cheek. There is a faint odd smell, like bad breath, coming off her. Or maybe I am imagining it. But I cannot touch her. I straighten up again, my heart hammering in my chest.

'It's all right, John Joe,' says the Ardmháistir. I'd forgotten about him. 'Remember the seashells Mary Brigid collected and put on the windowsills? They are beautiful but empty. The creatures that lived in them outgrew those shells and moved on.

'This is not really your mother any more, John Joe. Your mother has outgrown this world and gone to live with God. What you see now is only the shell she left behind. It cannot hurt you, and it's nothing to fear.'

The stone in my stomach softens just a little. I bend down again and kiss the cold white cheek goodbye.

I don't remember much else. That day is erased like words on a blackboard. The funeral and the cemetery are blurred in my mind as well. I was there, I know that much, and so was Mr Pearse, at least part of the time. And when it was over he brought me back to St Enda's.

I'll be spending Christmas at St Enda's and going to

Mass with the Pearse family. My father is closed in on himself, taking no interest in anything but drink. It was Aunt Nell's decision to let me stop here. I'm grateful to her. How dreadful it would be to spend the holidays amid covered mirrors and stopped clocks. And that awful cold room upstairs with the door closed.

The other day I found one of Mam's handkerchiefs in the pocket of my Norfolk jacket. She lent it to me a long time ago when I had a cold. The scrap of linen was wadded up and pushed so deep I had forgot about it. I'm always forgetting about things in my pockets.

Finding it was like receiving a message from Mam. I buried my nose in the old, soft linen and thought for a moment I could smell the scent she used. Like lilac blossoms. She used to love lilacs. When they bloomed in our back garden she brought armloads of blossom into the house. Once she put some in a vase in my room, but my father threw them out. He said boys shouldn't have flowers.

Where are you now, Mam? Don't you know how much I miss you? There's a great big hole in my life and nothing is going to fill it, not ever.

Roger and the other boys have all gone home for the holidays. Without them, St Enda's is full of echoes.

Mrs Pearse is making a great fuss over me. She means well, but she keeps reminding me of what I've lost and I don't need reminding. Fortunately Willie, as always, takes his lead from his brother, and lets me grieve in my own way. His sympathy is obvious, though. Willie's feelings show on his face, he makes no effort to hide them. My father would say that's unmanly.

I don't think so. I think Willie is very kind.

The Ardmháistir is not here very much. He attends meetings at all hours and returns with a light in his eyes as if a lamp were glowing inside him. How I envy him. Inside me it's very dark. I'm sure I shall never be happy again.

Christmas dinner is served in the family dining room, where a small tree has been decorated with ribbons and candles. Mary Brigid plays a harp accompaniment while her mother and sister bring in the food. I'm not very hungry. I manage to eat a sliver of turkey and a few bites of pudding and drink a glass of lemonade. Then I just want to go up to the dormitory and get into bed.

Mam's handkerchief is under my pillow.

When the Ardmháistir is away from the school Willie looks after me. Willie adores his brother and will do anything he asks of him, including giving up his own free time to try to lift my spirits. On the Saturday after Christmas he takes me into Dublin on the tram.

Grafton Street is thronged with shoppers. Shiny black motor cars nose their way through the crowds. Fuller's and Mitchell's are crowded with scores of young men and women ordering coffee, or sipping ice-cream sodas.

'Would you care for an ice-cream soda?' Willie asks.

A few weeks ago I would have turned handsprings for an ice-cream soda. I've only ever had one, on a day when Mam took me into the city for shopping. The last day Mam ever …

'No thank you, sir,' I say.

We wander up and down the pavement a while. Willie asks if I would like to go to the panto. 'If you want to,' I reply with a shrug. He drops the subject and buys a bag of sweets for me instead. I offer him the first one, of course, then eat one myself to be polite. Afterward I cram the paper bag into my coat pocket and forget about it.

We are back at the Hermitage in time for tea. Mrs Pearse serves a steak-and-kidney pie – my favourite – but I don't have any appetite. 'I must have eaten too many sweets,' I tell her.

Willie darts a glance at me but does not give me away.

Some time later I find the bag of sweets in my coat pocket. The coat was hung too close to the fire and they have melted into an awful lump.

In the first week of the new year Mr Pearse returns from one of his meetings in a state of excitement. He tells us, 'By the end of the year the Irish Volunteers had almost ten thousand men signed up! There is to be a female auxiliary as well, called Cumann na mBan.'

'What can women do?' I ask; thinking of my poor frail mother lying in her bed, so helpless …

'Without the support of the women the nationalist movement would be far weaker. They have their own quiet courage,' Mr Pearse asserts, adding, in a faraway voice as if he's thinking of someone special, 'and more grit than many men.'

Yesterday Countess Markievicz paid a call on Mr Pearse. This morning he summons me to his office. 'John Joe, the Fianna is growing rapidly. Boys who are too young to join the Volunteers are flocking to be members. How about you? It would give you something to take your mind off …' He does not finish. I knew what he means, and am grateful for the suggestion.

'I should like very much to join the Fianna, sir. But when I asked for permission before, I was told it would worry my mother.'

'It will not worry her now,' he says gently. 'Shall we try again?'

CHAPTER FIVE

MARCH 1914

In February the Ardmháistir went to America on a fund-raising tour for the school. Without his stern presence we might have run riot, but we did not. We boys worked harder at our lessons than ever so Willie would send him good reports of us. We redoubled our efforts at sports, too, and with the Fianna.

The St Enda's Company of Na Fianna Éireann is commanded by Con Colbert, who is a strict drill-master. No larking about is allowed. We form up in lines as straight as if drawn by a ruler, and we obey orders instantly. We have only rifles carved of wood for weapons drill. But when the order comes to shoulder arms every imitation weapon sits on every shoulder at the same precise angle.

The Fianna uniform includes a double-breasted dark green tunic with lots of useful pockets. The hat is the same as that of the Boy Scouts in Britain, but the Fianna badge is a gold sunburst with a white pikestaff head on a green field. For dress parade there is a saffron-coloured kilt like those Fionn's warriors wore. The first time I saw boys in kilts I started to laugh at them, but then I changed my mind. They looked ... proud. Before I came to St Enda's, my teachers told me the Irish were ignorant peasants with nothing to be proud of, but now I know that's wrong.

We had Cúchulainn and Fionn MacCumhaill and Brian Boru. And Mr Pearse says we have the future, too.

My uniform has been ordered from a woman in Dublin who makes them, but it hasn't arrived yet. With so many boys anxious to join there's quite a backlog. Roger's joined, too, and already has his uniform. In his new gear he doesn't seem pudgy, but sturdy, like a real soldier. So I tell him, 'You look a right pillock,' and he gives me a shove and I give him a shove.

I'm grateful to Aunt Nell for giving me permission to become one of the Fianna. I've heard nothing from my father, however. I suppose he's glad to be rid of me.

I don't care. I have the Pearses. And the future.

On the parade ground – which is also our playing

field – Commandant Colbert issues his commands in Irish. In the school's prospectus Mr Pearse states that St Enda's can turn a boy into a competent Irish speaker within a year. But I can understand Con Colbert already.

Countess Markievicz can shoot a rifle. She demonstrated it for us today and hit the bull's eye three times in a row. I never saw a woman shoot a rifle before. She is a wonder. She is an officer in James Connolly's Citizen Army, which is mostly composed of working-class people, and drills with them in Croydon Park. She also set up a soup kitchen in Liberty Hall, the headquarters of the trade union movement, for victims of the lockout. She spends part of every day working there, yet she still finds time to visit the various companies of the Fianna around Dublin. When the Countess comes to see us we step out smartly while she watches like a general reviewing his troops. A slight nod of approval from her makes us feel ten feet tall.

I think Madame – that's what we call her, she has no use for titles – should wear golden armour and brandish a great sword. For her sake I would storm the gates of Heaven. Or of Hell, though I'd never let Mr Pearse hear me say *that*.

He wants so much to believe that we are pure and good, filled with the high ideals he cherishes. The truth is, we sometimes have bad thoughts and do bad things. We are just boys.

Although boys enjoy a good scrap among themselves, in the Fianna we imagine a common enemy and are training to fight him together. There is a great spirit among the Fianna: *esprit de corps,* Madame calls it.

One afternoon on the playing field I offer to help Roger improve at hurling. In return, he invites me to come to his house and play with his dog. I'm going to do it, too! My father can't stop me playing with someone else's dog.

When Mam died I thought I would never have fun again. But I am having fun. Although sometimes I feel guilty, it's hard to feel guilty all the time.

In addition to drilling at the school we go on manoeuvres in the Dublin mountains with other Fianna companies. If the weather is not too bad, we bring a big trek cart to hold our supplies and tents and we camp out. Roger, who used to complain so bitterly about the cold, is one of the most eager campers.

Madame Markievicz personally leads the Fianna on marches through the streets of Dublin. We strut along the cobbles, past the blue and green gas lamps, with our heads up and our chests out and feeling as grown-up as anything. Madame points out historic sites such as the old Irish Parliament building – we no longer have a parliament of our own – and the place where Robert Emmet was hanged. We know all about Robert Emmet. We've been studying him in school, particularly his famous speech from the dock. Every time I read, 'When my country takes her place among the nations of the earth …' I get a lump in my throat.

The nationalist movement is gaining strength every day. Nationalists believe that Ireland should belong to her people and not to the British crown. The Ardmháistir and Willie Pearse and Thomas MacDonagh are all nationalists, and what they say makes sense to me.

Who is King George to tell us what to do? He's not even English, he's German, his family name is Saxe-Coburg-Gotha. I read that in the *Freeman's Journal* the other day. Willie goes out early every morning on his bicycle and brings back the newspapers, which we are encouraged to read.

My father never offered to let me read the papers. He said I wouldn't understand them. But I do. I understand when, on the twenty-fifth of April, the newspapers report that 35,000 rifles and 2 ½ million rounds of ammunition have been landed at Larne for the Ulster Volunteer Force.

Yet a recently passed law denies ordinary Irish men the right to bear arms. That's in the papers too.

A number of people who have nothing to do with

the school are paying calls on Mr Pearse. Sometimes the lights burn very late in his office, and from my dormitory window I can see large black motor-cars parked in the forecourt.

Between the playing field and the long drive that leads up to the house is a wide border of trees and shrubbery. There are a lot of laurels and rodosomethings that keep their leaves all year. When we leave the playing field we often take a short-cut through the border. This afternoon I stopped to whittle my initials – very small! – on a tree trunk, but before I finished I heard the bell ringing from the house to call us to tea. I dropped my knife into my coat pocket and began to run.

When I took off my coat to hang it up, the pocket was empty.

So here I am on hands and knees, searching the border for the knife my father gave me. His father gave it to him, and if I lose it – well, it doesn't bear thinking about.

I hear voices. The Ardmháistir and Mr MacDonagh are walking down the drive deep in conversation. I don't want Mr Pearse to know about me carving my initials, so I keep very still, trusting the leaves to hide me.

To my horror the two men stop only a few paces away. Can they hear the sudden pounding of my heart as I crouch here in the shrubbery? I say a quick prayer, promising God that if they don't find me I shall never eavesdrop again. Never ever.

'Things look very grave, Tom,' Mr Pearse is saying. 'According to today's papers, the UVF now claims to have over one hundred thousand men. They intend to set up what they call the 'provisional government of Ulster' if the Home Rule Bill passes in Parliament. It could mean another civil war.'

'My colleagues in Trinity are more concerned about the possibility of war in Europe,' Thomas MacDonagh replies. 'The arms race is proceeding headlong with no concern for the ultimate result. Austria, Germany, France, even Russia ... why, the whole place is a powder keg, Pat. Any spark might set it off. Just think how many Irish men are in the British army right now. For so many of our poor it's the only way they can earn a living and support their families. If there is war on the Continent thousands more will be recruited, or conscripted, to protect British interests there.'

'To fight for King George?' Mr Pearse's voice crackles with anger. 'It's *this* country our lads should be fighting for!'

'Ireland? Ireland's nothing more than a supplier of cannon fodder for Britain,' Mr MacDonagh says glumly. Although usually cheerful, he has melancholy moods. I suppose that's part of being a poet.

They begin walking again and pass out of my hearing. But those words echo in my ears. Cannon fodder for Britain.

I wait for a long time before going back to the house.

The Study Hall is a large, rectangular room in a wing off the main house. At the far end is a big pull-down map of the world. The British Empire, coloured a vivid pink, dominates. If we glance up from our desks it is the first thing we see.

To the right of the map is a doorway that leads to the Chapel. On one side of the room is a stage for our theatrical performances, on the other side are tall windows that look out onto the lawn. The March light coming into the hall is dull and grey, and I am squinting at my own handwriting, trying to make sense of the chicken tracks on my paper, when the Ardmháistir enters. His unexpected appearance comes as a surprise. We're not supervised in study hall because we're on our honour. We all stand up. Mr Pearse acknowledges our courtesy and gestures for us to sit down again. He goes to the map. Producing a small pot of paint and a brush, he begins to paint Ireland green.

It's the most defiant act I've ever seen.

Or is it? I almost remember something that happened when I was very small, a terrifying morning when …

no, it's slid away. I don't want to remember.

The boy sitting beside me today, Ned Halloran, is several years older than I and comes from the west of Ireland. While the rest of us gape at the Ardmháistir, Ned rises to his feet and puts his hand over his heart.

'The Republic of Ireland,' he says in a strong, clear voice.

A swift intake of breath, then we are all on our feet.

'The Republic of Ireland!'

CHAPTER SIX

JULY 1914

I'm spending the summer at home, but it's no holiday. My father either shouts and roars or is deadly
quiet, it's hard to know which is more dangerous.
When there's drink taken he slams his fist against the
wall and breaks the furniture. Some nights he does not
even come home. To make matters worse, he and Aunt
Nell are fighting worse than ever. I'm afraid she'll walk
out and leave me alone with my father.

At night I kneel beside my bed and pray to Mam,
asking her to help me. I know I should be praying to
Jesus and Mary and the saints, but the only face I see
behind my closed eyes is my mother's.

In June the nationalists stage their annual pilgrimage

to the grave of Wolfe Tone at Bodenstown, and the Fianna, led by Constance Markievicz, are invited to take part. I desperately want to go but I make the mistake of asking my father on a morning when he has a sore head.

'I won't have you consorting with nationalist rabble!' he roars. Then winces at the pain behind his eyes.

Good. I hope it really hurts.

Later the newspapers carry the story. The Irish Volunteers, the Citizen Army, Cumann na mBan and the Fianna all turned out for the event, which was huge. A notorious republican called Tom Clarke gave a ringing address at the graveside.

And I was sitting at home.

Mr MacDonagh was right.

On the twenty-eighth of June, Archduke Ferdinand of Austria and his wife were shot dead as they rode in their carriage. The assassin is a Serbian. I know where Serbia is; it's in the Balkans, one of the areas which is not pink on the map.

The killings have brought Austria and Serbia to the point of war. Britain has offered to mediate – which means try to make peace between the two – but the offer was rejected. The Kaiser of Germany condemned the British offer as 'insolence'. It's as if the great nations were just waiting for an excuse, like boys spoiling for a fight. The Russian Czar has mobilised his army. So have Germany and France.

Closer to home, the *Irish Press* reports the Ulster Volunteer Force marching through Belfast fully armed and carrying two Colt machine guns.

On the twenty-fifth of July a handwritten note addressed to me is delivered by a member of the Fianna. 'On Sunday next, Na Fianna Éireann will stage a joint exercise with the Irish Volunteers. Manoeuvres shall consist of a long route march originating in and returning to Dublin. Following early Mass please present yourself in uniform at Father Matthew Park in Fairview. Bring a day's rations.'

The Irish Volunteers have been holding route marches for weeks. If we've been invited to join them I'm determined not to miss it!

Instead of approaching my father I go to Aunt Nell. 'How far is Fairview from here?'

'Miles away on the north side, John Joe. It's land recently reclaimed from the estuary of the Liffey. Why are you interested?'

'The Fianna are holding an exercise there tomorrow after Mass. May I go? I can ride my bicycle.'

A mischievous light comes into her eyes. 'Very well, but you must be home by teatime. Let your father assume you've been playing with your friends.'

Aunt Nell and I are conspirators against my father.

On Sunday morning I dress as usual. Then I fold my Fianna uniform very tightly and stuff it into my backpack, together with a cheese sandwich and an apple. Aunt Nell and I attend Mass together. My father never goes to church any more. When the service is over I set out for Fairview, pausing long enough to change clothes in the toilet of a hotel on the quays. Several people are sitting in the hotel lobby reading the Sunday papers. When I come out wearing my Fianna uniform, the desk clerk tells them, 'That's one of the Countess's boys.'

I cannot resist swaggering a bit as I leave the hotel.

Father Matthew Park is little more than a waste-ground with a few straggling bushes. By the time I arrive the place is already crowded with men and boys. Bicycles belonging to the Volunteer Cycle and Signalling Corps are lying on the ground to one side, so I leave my bicycle with the rest and start looking for someone I know.

Mr MacDonagh and Ned Halloran are standing with Éamonn Ceannt, who has played music for us at the school. All three wear grey-green Volunteer uniforms with Sam Browne belts and peaked caps. Most of the men here are in civilian clothes, however. They have done the best they can by belting their coats tightly around their waists and wrapping canvas around their shins to look like leggings.

A familiar voice shouts my name. 'John Joe!' Roger is running toward me. 'This is some hooley! What did you bring for rations?'

'Cheese sandwiches and an apple. You?'

He pats the various pockets of his tunic. 'Buttered scones, fruit cake, a bottle of minerals, and three packs of chocolate biscuits.'

'You better hope that butter doesn't melt in your pocket. Do you know where we're going?'

Roger looks smug, the way he does when he knows something I don't. 'Out to Howth and back.'

'How far is that?'

'Miles and miles,' he says casually, which means he doesn't really know. 'I brought a change of socks anyway.'

I did not think to bring a change of socks, but I'm not going to tell Roger that.

Con Colbert strides briskly toward us. He's wearing his Fianna uniform with a Volunteer badge pinned to the tunic. 'Glad you two could come, that gives us a full complement from St Enda's. I won't be your commandant today, though. You'll take your orders from Bulmer Hobson.'

'How many men are here altogether, sir?'

He sweeps the crowd with his eyes. 'Eight companies of the Dublin Brigade and almost a hundred Fianna. Nine hundred in total, I'd say.'

'Nine hundred,' Roger murmurs, sounding impressed. He points to the Fianna trek cart, which is parked off to one side. 'Do we have enough refreshments for so many?'

'Can you lads keep a secret?' We both nod, of course. 'Well, today that cart's loaded with weapons of self-defence in case the police try to stop us.'

In case the police try to stop us? What sort of march is this?

As soon as Con Colbert leaves us to join his comrades in the Dublin Brigade, I suggest we look inside the cart. Roger pulls up a corner of the tarp while I peek beneath. The cart's filled to the brim with stout oak batons!

Just then Bulmer Hobson gives the order to form up. The Fianna are to march in the middle of the column, surrounded by Volunteers. The big trek cart, pulled by a team of Fianna, will bring up the rear. Since Roger and I happen to be standing near the cart, we're among the boys assigned to the team.

It's not always smart to be curious. I can't help it, though.

The column sets off at a spanking pace. With the heavily

laden trek cart, we're pushed to the pins of our collars to keep up. Fortunately the teams are rotated frequently.

People hang out of their windows to watch the march go by. Some of them laugh and applaud. I feel like laughing myself, I've never had so much fun in my life.

As we move out into the countryside a strong wind begins to blow off the Irish Sea. The sun was shining earlier but clouds are gathering now. Although the temperature is dropping I'm not cold. I swing along with my chin up and my shoulders back as if Madame herself were watching. Roger is already eating the food he brought. I don't want to open my pack while we're marching. It would not look very soldierly.

Clontarf, Dollymount, Raheny, Kilbarrack, Sutton. We pass small cottages and large country houses, sheep in pens and horses in pasture, fields of corn and vegetable plots. The Hill of Howth rises ahead of us like the shoulder of a giant emerging from Dublin Bay.

I'm getting a blister on my heel but I'm not going to limp. I don't cry and I don't limp.

We're almost in Howth when the order is given to halt. 'About bloody time,' Roger mutters. He's out of breath at this stage. We've marched about eight miles, I guess, without a break. I'm breathing hard myself but I keep my mouth closed so it doesn't show.

The Fianna are summoned to the front of the column by an officer called Cathal Brugha, whom I recognise because he's been to St Enda's a couple of times. 'We need nimble lads who can move quickly,' he tells us, 'so the next part of the operation is up to you. We'll be following this road on into the village. The harbour will be on your left. When a yacht called the *Asgard* arrives you are to go aboard as soon as she docks, and unload her cargo. Don't waste a minute. Once the goods are ashore the Volunteers will take charge of them.'

Roger and I exchange glances. He lifts his eyebrows. 'Unload cargo?'

'It's no worse,' I reply, 'than being a draft horse for a trek cart.'

The march resumes. Some of the Volunteers were singing earlier, but they're tired now, and quiet by the time we enter the village. To our left a forest of masts rises from the water. Lobster pots are stacked on the stone quay fronting the harbour. The air smells sharp and salty. Gulls shriek overhead. One drops a great white splodge on the shoulder of the boy in front of me, but I don't tell him. Instead I nudge Roger and we grin silently.

Three large motor cars pass us at speed. They park along the quay. Several men in long coats get out and begin walking back and forth, gazing out toward

Ireland's Eye. Fishermen who are spreading their nets to dry watch them curiously.

Since I've never been to Howth before I want to see everything. My head swivels around to look at the little boats bobbing like corks on the water, the cottages scattered across the hill, the sweet shop with a row of glass jars in the window …

'No time for gawking, lads,' Bulmer Hobson calls out. 'Take possession of the pier now. Step lively!'

We trot smartly onto the timber pier and form two lines. Behind us on the quay, the Volunteers wait impatiently. There's a lot of foot-shifting and milling about. Obviously they aren't as well-drilled as we are.

Spectators are gathering on the hillside above us. What do they expect to see? There is a tingling in the air like the atmosphere before thunder. I don't know just what's going to happen but something is, something big, something exciting.

We are barely in position when one of the men in long coats gives a shout. 'It's the harbinger of liberty!' He points to a sleek little yacht beating its way toward Howth against the rising gale. It seems to be very low in the water. As the yacht draws nearer we can make out two women among the small crew on deck.

Glancing around, I see Mr MacDonagh talking with

the men in long coats. His face is flushed and his eyes are very bright.

From the far side of the harbour a coast guard vessel flying the Union Jack sets out to meet the yacht. I hold my breath, I'm not sure why. They turn back when they see how many men are gathered at quayside. There are only four or five men on the coast guard boat and almost a thousand of us.

Several taxicabs have arrived by now, and parked on the quay. They leave their motors running.

After skilful manoeuvring to avoid the fishing boats, the yacht reaches the pier. It almost overshoots, but as the lines are thrown out a couple of the Volunteers make a valiant effort to catch them and pull the yacht back. In a couple of minutes the vessel is securely docked. The Fianna in the front row – including Roger and me – quickly go aboard.

When I jump down onto the deck I can feel the yacht sway like a living thing. My stomach comes right up into my throat. But there's no time to be queasy. The hatches have been removed and we can see the cargo waiting for us below.

The penny drops.

The *Asgard* is packed with rifles for the Irish Volunteers!

A man in oilskins identifies himself as Erskine

Childers, the captain of the yacht, and very politely thanks us for coming. He helps the two women onto the pier, then he and three other men disembark.

Meanwhile some of the Fianna go below. They find the saloon-cabin and passageway almost blocked by stacks of guns, taking up every conceivable inch of space. More are piled onto the bunks and stowed in the lockers. 'They've put their mattresses down on the guns and been sleeping on them!' a boy shouts to those of us on deck.

They begin handing the weapons out to us through the hatches. As the first rifles appear, some of the Volunteers break ranks and rush forward, shoving the Fianna on the pier aside in their eagerness to get to the guns. It's awfully dangerous; one boy is almost knocked into the water between the pier and the boat.

Erskine Childers shouts, 'There'll be no unloading until someone takes command of those men!'

An extremely tall, bespectacled officer is the first to bring his company under control. He uses his voice like a whiplash. Shame-faced, the Volunteers fall back.

'That man is a friend of my parents,' Roger boasts. 'He's a maths teacher called de Valera.'

With order restored, we begin handing the weapons up to the Fianna on the pier. The spectators on the hillside cheer! The operation goes with amazing smoothness, every boy doing his part. By passing them hand to hand along the column, nine hundred rifles and several boxes of ammunition are unloaded in half an hour.

My arms and shoulders ache and my hands are filthy with grease. If I were not wearing my Fianna uniform I would wipe my hands on my clothes. Instead I wipe them on one of the lines securing the *Asgard* to the pier. I suppose a little grease won't hurt a piece of wet rope.

The Volunteers pack the rifles into the waiting taxi-cabs, which roar away toward the city as soon as they are loaded. A number of the Volunteers keep rifles for themselves.

But the ammunition boxes are still sitting on the quay.

Bulmer Hobson calls us to him. 'It appears the Fianna are the only ones who have enough discipline to be entrusted with ammunition. Empty out the trek cart and put these boxes into it. They're your responsibility now.'

Are we proud!

In double-quick time we've emptied the cart of batons and stacked the wooden ammo boxes inside.

The spectators on the hill, the private motor cars, the heavily-laden taxicabs – all disappear within a matter of minutes. By the time we leave Howth it looks just like the sleepy little fishing village it was when we arrived.

Yet everything is different now.

CHAPTER SEVEN

JULY 1914, SURREY HOUSE

With Mr MacDonagh in the lead, we march back toward Dublin even more swiftly than we came out. Officers move up and down the column, taking the names of the men who grabbed rifles for themselves. I overhear one officer say sternly, 'Either hand over that rifle at the next meeting of your company, or pay for it in weekly instalments.'

We keep up a hard pace until we reach Raheny. Our work done, the party of Fianna is bringing up the rear. At Raheny the column stops for a short break. Poor Roger is gasping like a fish out of water and he's not the only one. Our rest is far too short and then we're off again. By now it's a matter of gritting my teeth and keeping my head down. Refusing to give up. I have a dreadful stitch in my side but I will not give up. Roger, bless him, is as stubborn as I am. We won't disgrace ourselves.

As we near Clontarf there's a commotion up ahead. I'm craning my neck but I can't see what's going on. Then one of the Cycle Corps comes pedalling back along the column, shouting, 'The police and the soldiers were waiting for us with fixed bayonets! Get the Fianna boys away!'

Our party swerves off the main road and makes for the Malahide Road. Just our luck – Roger and I are on cart duty again. We trundle after the others as fast as we can.

We have hardly gone a hundred yards when we hear gunshots. The Volunteers at the front of the column are clashing with the police.

We proceed a few hundred yards more while the din grows worse. Rifle shots and revolver shots and at least one scream of pain. Some of our boys break ranks and run back the way they have come, unable to resist joining in the fray. I'm about to go with them when an officer cries, 'Save the ammunition at all costs!'

Roger stands there with his mouth open but my brain is racing.

We can't run far dragging the cart. With a rock from the roadside I smash open one of the boxes and begin stuffing the ammunition into my clothing. The nearest boys join in.

Soon a score of us are positively clanking with metal. Leaving the cart behind, we scramble down into a ditch and head across an open field. Many of the Volunteers are fleeing too, trying to save their weapons. I see one man who is bleeding badly as he stumbles along.

We come to a laneway that leads to a big country house almost hidden by a high hedge. Some of the boys turn in there to bury their ammunition in the grounds. I think we're still too close, so I keep running.

If Roger was huffing and puffing before, he's in a desperate state now. I can hear him floundering along behind me but I keep on. My only thought is to save the ammunition.

'Where are we going?' Roger croaks at last.

I have to stop to take bearings. We are eight boys alone in the middle of unfamiliar countryside. Since this was my idea the others are looking to me as their leader. For a moment I'm scared; I don't know how to be a commander.

The continuing sound of gunfire carries clearly across the open fields.

'I think we'd best deliver this ammunition to Madame,' I decide. 'She'll know what to do with it.'

Surrey House, in Dublin, is Madame's town residence, although she also has a small cottage in the country. She once marched us past Surrey House so I know where it is. It will be a long walk, tired as we are. I wish I could return to Fairview and collect my bicycle but I dare not.

A steady rain begins to fall.

By the time we reach Madame's house we are all desperately weary. There are lights in the windows, but suppose no one is home? I have no idea what we will do then. Getting us here is all I can manage.

The knocker makes a thunderous sound. Almost at once there is a quick, light footstep inside and the door opens. Madame herself is standing there, looking out with surprise at what appear to be eight very fat Fianna boys. She brings us into the sitting room. There is a comfortable-looking couch in a big bow window and a fire burning brightly in the fireplace. Warming themselves by the fire are Nora Connolly, James Connolly's daughter, and a troop of Irish Girl Guides, sort of like a female Fianna. The girls burst into giggles at the sight of us.

I wave my arm in the air as if brandishing a rifle. 'Guess what we've been doing!'

'It's too much trouble to guess,' Madame says. 'Tell us about it and we'll know all the quicker.'

The story comes tumbling out of me then, with constant interruptions and additions from the other boys. Except for Roger, who has discovered a tray of pastries.

The girls are camping out in Madame's back garden. When the rain got too heavy they came inside – and then we arrived. We are treated like heroes and immediately given cups of sweet, hot tea. Madame insists we take off our wet boots and socks, and after we unload our bulging pockets, Miss Connolly spreads our tunics before the fire to dry. I feel like a feather without all that ammunition weighing me down. I'm positively light headed.

Perhaps that's why I don't notice at first that Madame seems distracted. She goes to the door several times and peers out. When the telephone rings somewhere inside she almost trips over a footstool in her haste to answer. She returns wearing a deep frown, but forces a smile when she sees me watching.

'I think you boys deserve a party.' Madame glances toward the pastry tray, but Roger has left only crumbs. 'Nora, will you fetch some minerals from the pantry and set your girls to making sandwiches? When that's done we shall need pallets made up for these lads, they're spending the night here.'

'I can't possibly,' I protest, 'I'm expected at home.'

'I'm sure you all are, but I prefer that you stay with me until morning. Dublin is not a safe place tonight.'

Madame can be very firm. We do not argue.

'I'm glad you're staying,' one of the Girl Guides tells me. She is small and thin, with a great mass of curly hair tied back from her face by a ribbon. 'It was pretty boring until you boys arrived.'

'I shouldn't think one would ever be bored with Madame.'

'Oh, not her. But some of the other girls are very silly. They don't like sleeping in a tent because they're afraid of spiders.'

'What's your name?' I ask.

'Marcella.'

'Are you not afraid of spiders, Marcella?'

She tosses her head with a laugh. Her ringlets bounce up and down like bedsprings. 'Let the spiders be afraid of me!'

When the rain has passed the girls are sent back to their tents in the garden. Marcella gives me a wink as she goes out the door. She holds up one hand with the fingers bent like spiders' legs. I can't help laughing.

We boys remain settled in front of the fire. Already

our adventure seems like something that happened to someone else – except for the dreadful blister on my heel. I dread putting on my boots in the morning.

There are more telephone calls, then a couple of men come to the door. They hold a low-voiced conversation with Madame but do not enter the house.

After talking with them, Madame looks more grave than ever.

I have to ask. 'It's bad, isn't it?'

'It *is* bad, John Joe. None of the Volunteers was killed, as far as I know, though a number were injured. But there's been a massacre at Bachelor's Walk.'

'What!'

'The Dublin police and the soldiers – the King's Own Scottish Borderers – failed to disarm the Volunteers, who escaped with almost all of the weapons. The troops had to return to town empty-handed. News of their failure reached the city ahead of them. A great crowd gathered to heckle them: men, women, even small children. The King's Own made their way along the quays toward their barracks in the Phoenix Park, then stopped and took up a position at the Ha'penny Bridge. The heckling was out of hand by then. The soldiers fired on the crowd. Four people were killed and dozens have been taken to hospital.'

'The soldiers fired on innocent civilians?'

Madame narrows her lips into a thin line. 'Oh yes,' she says. 'Oh yes.'

Madame sends word to our parents that we are staying the night with her. I don't think I can possibly fall asleep, but the next thing I know a bright sun is streaming through the windows.

After breakfast Madame announces that she will take us home herself.

I explain that I need to go to Father Matthew Park to collect my bicycle. 'I shall take you there, then,' she replies, 'and you can ride your cycle home. Or we can carry it in my car if you like.'

What could be more wonderful than being driven to my own house in the motor-car of Countess Markievicz?

Unfortunately my father is at work and does not see my triumphal arrival. But Aunt Nell does. She dithers around waving her hands in the air and saying things like 'Your Ladyship' until finally Madame takes pity on her. 'Eleanor, my friends call me Con and I hope you will too.'

Aunt Nell turns a bright red. 'Oh I couldn't!' But as Madame is taking her leave, she manages to stammer, 'Thank you so much for your kindness to John Joe, Your La ... I mean, Con.'

I suspect my aunt will drop references to 'her friend Con' in every conversation from now on.

With the exception of the *Freeman's Journal*, all the newspapers express outrage at what they call 'an unprovoked attack on authority by a gang of armed outlaws'. As for the killings on Bachelor's Walk, that is recounted in a way which makes the Volunteers sound as if they were to blame.

That night at the dinner table my father is ranting about the vicious criminal element who call themselves the Irish Volunteers.

I glance at my aunt. She says nothing, but keeps her gaze fixed on the plate in front of her.

A month to the day after the assassination of the archduke, Austria declares war on Serbia.

On the first of August, the Kaiser declares war on the Czar. And at Kilcoole in County Wicklow a boat called the *Kelpie* lands more rifles for the Irish Volunteers. It's reported toward the back of the *Irish Times*. The gathering storm in Europe is on the front page.

Two days later the Kaiser declares war on France.

The little nation of Belgium lies in the way of a German advance into France. Britain has a treaty with Belgium, promising to protect the smaller country in the event of aggression.

The British have never honoured their treaties with us.

In my room is a calendar advertising Sunlight Soap. Every morning I mark off the number of days left until I can go back to St Enda's. On the fifth of August I mark off the day, then go downstairs for my breakfast. Aunt Nell is sitting at the table with the *Irish Times* spread in front of her. She looks up at me with tragic eyes. 'Germany invaded Belgium yesterday, John Joe. Britain has declared war on the Kaiser.'

Every day I strike off the calendar brings more bad news. Austria declares war on Russia, Serbia declares war on Germany, Germany and Austria threaten to attack Italy if it tries to remain neutral. Russia declares war on Germany. Events come thick and fast and seem to make no sense at all.

When I ask Aunt Nell if she understands what's going on, she shakes her head and clucks her tongue. 'It's terribly sad, John Joe. Queen Victoria's sons and daughters married into all the great royal courts of Europe. The English King and the German Kaiser are first cousins and the Russian Czarina is Victoria's granddaughter. Just a few years ago they were the best of friends, they went on holidays together. Look at them now. Thousands of men are going to die for the sake of what is, after all, a family squabble.'

A family squabble. We know about those, in this house.

Colourful recruiting posters appear on hoardings, urging men to sign up for the British army. 'Free Belgium and Serbia from the Hun!' 'Join the Fight on Behalf of Small Nations!'

One Saturday night my father bumps into me on the stair. He stumbles back, the smell of drink off him as thick as muck. When he raises one hand I draw back before I can stop myself. I know it's a mistake, that always makes him worse.

Instead of hitting me, he laughs. A sneering, snarling laugh. 'They're claiming this war will be over by Christmas,' he says, 'but for your sake I hope it lasts longer. Military service would do you a power of good.'

If I ever do fight I want to fight for Ireland. This is a small country too.

The following day, Aunt Nell and my father have a dreadful row at dinner. In the finish-up he grabs the table cloth and hurls our entire meal onto the floor. The bacon and cabbage, the roast potatoes, the fragrant brown gravy … and I haven't had a chance to take a bite yet.

My aunt pushes back her chair and gets to her feet. Her face is as tightly closed as a shuttered window. 'That's done it, Bertie. Ye've seen the last of me in this house.'

'You can't!' my father cries. 'What about the boy?'

'You should have thought of that sooner. I strongly suggest you ring the school and ask the Pearses to take him before the autumn term begins.'

What bliss to be back at St Enda's! This time I have been allowed to bring my bicycle with me, since there is no fear I might run away. Having my own transportation makes me feel more independent.

Mrs Pearse lets me help her prepare for the return of the other students. They will be here in a couple of weeks so there's a lot to be done. We sweep and dust and scrub, boil sheets, beat rugs, polish windows and mirrors, take an inventory of the pantry. I've never done any of those things before. At home I would scorn them. Here it's an honour. Besides, Mr Pearse says a man should be able to turn his hand to anything.

'When it's time to boil the Christmas puddings perhaps you may help me again, John Joe,' his mother suggests. 'I shall need someone strong to tie up the puddings in the pudding cloth, and my boys are so busy these days.'

Someone strong. That's me!

On the last day of August there is a terrible bloodbath at a place called Mons. That's in Belgium; I look at the map to be sure. The British forces begin to pull back. Afterward, some of them claim they saw a shining angel that halted the advance of the German cavalry long enough to allow them to get away. I ask Mr Pearse if that's possible. 'Miracles are always possible,' he says.

The war's spreading. The Emperor of Japan has declared war on Germany.

'I thought the war was a family squabble,' I remark to Mr Pearse.

He laughs. 'Perhaps that's how it started, but in the finish-up all wars are about territory, John Joe. When this one's over they'll have to redraw the maps.'

'Is that a bad thing or a good thing, sir?'

'It might be a good thing,' he says slowly. 'It just might be. Have you ever heard the saying, 'England's trouble is Ireland's opportunity'?'

I read in the newspapers that hundreds of men are joining the Irish Volunteers now. I wonder if we have enough guns for all of them.

CHAPTER EIGHT

SEPTEMBER 1914

All the students have returned to St Enda's, and the war is being fought at sea as well as on land. It is even in the sky, with aeroplanes duelling above the clouds like knights of old. That sounds pretty exciting to me. On Sunday afternoon Mr MacDonagh reads to us from 'The Idylls of the King', which is not Irish, but English, and about King Arthur and the Knights of the Round Table. Afterward we discuss chivalry and codes of honour.

In tales of chivalry there are Fair Ladies who give the knights their colours to wear. Scarves, I suppose that means. I would feel silly asking a girl for her scarf, until I remember the silk ribbon Marcella used to hold back her curls. It was a plain dark blue, something I could tie around my sleeve without feeling ridiculous.

I like to imagine myself as a knight in armour, riding out on a prancing charger to have adventures. There are no more dragons to slay – at least I don't think so – but there are always battles to fight.

The Prime Minister calls for 500,000 more men to join the British army. The Empire rallies to the colours. Regiments from Ireland embark for the Continent, while Canada, Australia and New Zealand prepare to send expeditionary forces.

'Brave Men must be willing to die for King and Country!' shout the posters on the hoardings.

But which country? Theirs? Or our own?

Any possibility of the Home Rule Act being passed has vanished now. It is suspended for the duration of the war.

Roger's two older brothers, James and Donald, have enlisted in the Dublin Fusiliers. He's very proud of them; there's a big photograph of them in their uniforms on top of his locker. After about the tenth time Roger boasts about his wonderful amazing incredible brothers, I lose my temper. 'Your brothers are stupid to fight for King George.'

'My brothers are not stupid! And why shouldn't they fight for the king? We're British after all.'

'Remember what we learned in history? Ireland was

free for thousands of years before the English set out to conquer this island. They call themselves the British Empire now, but *this*,' I stamp my foot on the ground, 'is still Ireland, and you and I and our parents and their parents were all born *here*. We're Irish!'

Roger isn't the sort to back down. 'We're British!' he insists, glaring at me.

I'm not one to back down either. 'If you think that you're as bloody stupid as your bloody brothers. Rome conquered France and Germany and Spain but that didn't make the people who lived there into Romans!'

Roger and I have a fight in back of the handball court. It isn't much of a fight, but he thumps me and I thump him until Michael MacRory catches us and marches us into the Ardmháistir's office.

Mr Pearse asks, 'Is the fight over now?'

We both nod. Even if it's not true.

'Then shake hands.'

We keep our hands in our pockets.

Mr Pearse sits behind his desk watching us. Looking patient.

This is boring. I won't shake hands and I don't know what else is expected of me.

'Permission to leave the room, sir.'

'Permission denied, John Joe.'

So we stand here. I'm staring out the window and

Roger's staring at his feet. The only sound in the room is the ticking of the clock on the mantelpiece behind the Ardmháistir's desk.

After a while I begin to feel foolish. I cut my eyes at Roger and see that he is biting his lip.

The clock keeps ticking. We hear the distant clatter of pots and pans in the kitchen, then the eager voices of the other boys coming in for their tea.

My stomach embarrasses me by growling.

More time passes.

Mr Pearse opens one of the many books on his desk. He riffles through the pages, then clears his throat and begins to read aloud. 'Chieftains in ancient Ireland gave one another gifts after a battle, so their conflict would not continue into the next generation.'

I give Roger some of my best marbles, including a bulls-eye and two steelies. He gives me his leather belt with a wolfhound on the buckle.

Willie Pearse is appearing in a play by Chekov at the Irish Theatre in Hardwicke Street, which is managed by Mr MacDonagh. The play is quite sombre, I understand, but the Ardmháistir says his brother is wonderful in the part. He brings some of the St Enda's boys, myself included, to a matinee performance of the play. I'm seated next to Roger. Mr Pearse says, 'I hope you two won't mind sitting together?'

'Why should we mind?' Roger replies. 'Sure are we not friends?'

And we are.

CHAPTER NINE

DECEMBER 1914

On the second of December several nationalist newspapers are 'suppressed', meaning the government won't allow them to be published any more. The Ardmháistir is angry about it.

My father works in the department which has responsibility for things like suppressing newspapers, I'm ashamed to say.

Sometimes I pretend I'm an orphan. I almost am. My only happy memories of home date from the time when Mam was still alive and well. Is it possible that our house was a cheerful place then? I like to think it was, but maybe my memory is playing tricks on me. Maybe it was just Mam who was cheerful, and my father was always … No. I don't want to think about that.

The other boys have gone home for Christmas but I am still here. My father sends the money for my fees, but otherwise I am dumped like a dog dumped in the street. Since he's so set against Irish nationalism I'm surprised he leaves me at St Enda's. I suppose he's never made any serious enquiries into the nature of this school. It's enough for him that someone's willing to take me off his hands.

Meanwhile the Great War – that's what they're calling it now, since there has never been a conflict on this scale before – has bogged down in the trenches. The papers tell horror stories of mud and blood and ice all mixed together. Roger must be desperately worried about his brothers. I pray for them every day in chapel.

A most strange thing has happened.

On the Western Front the ordinary soldiers in the trenches declared a Christmas Truce of their own without permission from the generals. British and German soldiers met between the lines and exchanged jam and cigarettes. The generals are furious at their men for taking matters in their own hands.

If no one was willing to fight there wouldn't be any wars.

But what can one do when one's country is attacked?

Or dominated by a foreign power?

I'd like to ask the Ardmháistir but he's out for the day, attending a meeting of the Irish Republican Brotherhood, another nationalist organisation to which he belongs. It's a secret society. I would not know anything about the Brotherhood if I had not overheard a conversation between the Ardmháistir and Willie.

I don't earwig on purpose. I simply have a gift for being in the right place at the right time, and if interesting things are said within earshot, I can keep very still.

The Ardmháistir has left Willie in charge today. 'I'm relying on you to help me mind the place,' Willie says to me.

'I will of course!' I can see myself marching bravely down to the front gates to stand on guard with my wooden rifle on my shoulder, like one of the policemen outside Dublin Castle.

Willie Pearse is following in his father's footsteps as a monumental sculptor. He has fitted out a studio here with his father's old tools and equipment and has received several commissions. Since I'm the only student here now, he's invited me to come along and have a look. It's a great honour. Willie's very modest about his work and shy about showing it to anyone.

As I open the door to the studio I'm surprised to see other people already inside. Just then the stone dust in the air makes me sneeze. When I open my eyes again, the figures I mistook for living people are statues. Two large figures in marble are destined for churches down the country. One is the Dead Christ, the other, the Immaculate Conception. Every detail conveys Willie's reverence for his subject. There are a number of studies of children, too. Laughing boys and pretty girls and one tiny wee infant tenderly cradled in adult hands. All are so lifelike I expect to see them move.

'Why, these are amazing, Willie!'

He ducks his chin and looks embarrassed. 'Not at all, not at all.'

'But they are, they're beautiful. I didn't know you were so good.' I immediately bite my tongue. That sounded insulting.

Willie doesn't take offence. 'I learned the basics in my father's studio, then studied at the Metropolitan School of Art in Dublin and in Paris as well, for a while,' – his voice takes on a dreamy tone – 'that lovely city of lime-white palaces.'

All at once I understand what 'lyrical' means.

Willie has exhibited his sculpture at the Hibernian Academy and elsewhere and won numerous awards. Yet you would never know it to look at him. Like the Ardmháistir, he keeps everything inside.

I ask Willie the question my father would ask: 'Can

one make a living as an artist?'

'Art *is* living, John Joe. Trying to earn money with it is something else entirely. I only wish it did pay well, the school needs the money.'

The school is everything to the Pearse brothers. That, and Ireland.

When the Ardmháistir returns I ask him my question about war. He says, 'War is a terrible thing but war is not an evil thing. It is the things that make war necessary that are evil. You've heard me speak of James Connolly? Mr Connolly has written that just wars should be fought in, and unjust wars should be fought against.'

I shall be glad when the holidays are over and Roger comes back to school. I find myself worrying about his brothers as if they were my own. I have no brothers; I was going to have a little sister. But now I never will.

If I were really an orphan I wonder if Roger's parents would be willing to adopt me. I suppose I'd have to become a Protestant. Would that be so difficult? Mr Pearse is a devoted Catholic, but he says we all worship the same God anyway.

On the day Roger returns to St Enda's he and I have another fight, but it's sort of a pretend one. I'm so glad to see him I give him a really hard punch on the arm and he gets mad. So we flail away at each other for a while. Afterward we go into the kitchen together to ask Mrs Pearse for some bread and butter.

'How did you get that bruise on your face, Roger?' she wants to know.

He glances at me. 'I fell down.'

'All on your own? You simply fell down?'

'Well, we were running and … and this big dog ran out in front of us and … '

'What big dog? Here on the grounds? Should I ask Michael MacRory to go out and find it?'

'Unh, I threw a stone at it and it ran away,' says Roger.

She frowns. 'You threw a stone at an animal? Roger, I'm ashamed of you!'

'I mean we threw a stone at it. John Joe and me. John Joe more than me, actually.'

There was no big dog. When Roger starts lying he doesn't know how to stop, and he's going to get us both in trouble. Me more than him, actually. If he would just tell the truth we could stop this before it gets any worse. But he's not going to, he's getting that sulky look he gets some times. And I can't very well accuse my best friend of lying. Especially since he lied in the first place to keep from saying I hit him.

So here we are in the Ardmháistir's office again. He

looks at us, shakes his head, and gives a long sigh. 'What is it this time, boys? My mother says you've been up to something but she's not sure what. Surely you weren't fighting again.'

'We were not fighting, sir,' I say quickly. He would be so disappointed, after the last time, if … now I'm lying too. How did this happen?

There is only one thing for it. I take a very deep breath. This is terribly hard, I wish he would not look at me so trustingly.

Maybe that's why I have to do it.

'We were fighting, sir. Just roughhousing, you know. But when I hit Roger under the eye it made a bruise, and of course Mrs Pearse noticed it, and …'

'And I told a lie to keep John Joe from getting into trouble,' Roger interrupts gallantly.

'I see. And there was no dog?'

'No dog, sir. And no stone thrown at one, either.'

'Please sir,' says Roger, sounding very nervous, 'are we going to be punished?'

'Do you think you should be?'

Roger bites his lip.

'And you, John Joe, do you think you should be punished?'

Perhaps sometimes telling the truth can go too far. But having begun I must continue. 'I do think we should be punished, sir. We both told lies.'

The Ardmháistir's face fills with a light like the rising sun. He murmurs, 'Whatever else I may do with my life … ' He does not finish the thought. 'Thank you, boys, that will be all.'

Roger asks anxiously, 'What is our punishment, sir?'

'No punishment,' says Mr Pearse.

CHAPTER TEN

SPRING 1915

The Great War goes on and on and gets worse and worse. Germany has placed a submarine blockade around the British Isles. Zeppelin airships have dropped bombs on English towns.

Death falling silently out of the skies to kill innocent civilians.

In ancient Ireland battles were fought hand to hand. If you killed someone – or he killed you – you looked in each other's eyes first.

The Irish Volunteers have seven commanding officers in Dublin: Thomas MacDonagh, Joseph Plunkett (he edits *The Irish Review* and his father's the director of the Museum of Science and Art), Éamonn Ceannt,

Bulmer Hobson, Edward Daly (Tom Clarke's brother-in-law), Éamon de Valera, and our own Mr Pearse.

Willie teases his brother by calling him 'Commandant' and saluting him at inappropriate times. I don't think Mr Pearse would take it from anyone else, but when Willie does it he laughs.

With so many new Volunteers, the officers are kept busy trying to train them. Mr Pearse has organised a mock battle for the newest recruits to the Dublin Brigade. It will be held in the Dublin mountains on Easter Sunday.

'Why Easter Sunday, sir?' I want to know.

'Joe Plunkett suggested it. He likes the symbolism of the Resurrection.'

A small party of the St Enda's Fianna will accompany the Easter Sunday drill. I'm one of those chosen. Roger is not.

He is lying face down on his bed, making snuffling noises. He wouldn't want me to know he's crying, but I can't leave him like that. 'Everything all right?' I ask as cheerfully as I can.

He rolls over and looks up at me. His face is red and blotchy and his eyes are swimming. 'Nothing's all right. You're good at everything and I'm not good at anything. My parents talk about James and Donald all the time and they never talk about me.'

'You're good at lots of things,' I say loyally.

'Name three.'

'Well, Latin. You're good at Latin, much better than I am.'

'How wonderful for me.' He rolls over again and buries his face in his pillow.

Mr Pearse and Willie are in the Ardmháistir's office. When they see me standing in the open doorway the Ardmháistir snaps, 'What is it, John Joe?'

He's never short with the boys. He must have a lot on his mind.

'I was wondering, sir. About Roger?'

'What about Roger?'

'He's heartbroken at not being chosen for the Easter Sunday manoeuvres. Could you possibly add his name to the list? It would mean a lot to him, sir.'

In a kindlier voice, Mr Pearse says, 'The ground we'll be covering is very rough and we'll need our most athletic boys. Con Colbert tells me that Roger is not up to it. I'm sorry.'

'But he can do it, sir, I know he can! And if he has difficulties I'll help him.'

'This won't be a game, John Joe.' He drops his voice slightly. 'It's a rehearsal.'

'A rehearsal?' I don't understand. 'For a play, sir?'

'Not for a play.'

Once again the penny drops. It takes me a long time but eventually I get there. 'The Volunteers are not *just* to protect us, are they, sir? We'll be rehearsing for an uprising!'

Padraic Pearse does not answer but there is no need. I can see it in his face.

I can feel it in the leap of my heart.

An uprising, a rebellion against the British like the Rising of 1798! In my own lifetime. For a moment I can hardly breathe.

Then the thought comes to me: it won't be nearly as much fun if Roger's not there.

'Please sir, if you want me, take Roger as well. He can do it, I promise.'

Mr Pearse turns to his brother. 'What do you think, Willie?'

'I think I'd be very unhappy if you went without me.'

'Roger? Roger! Get up. You'll be going with us on Sunday.'

He raises his head and gives me a sour look. 'Who says?'

'The Ardmháistir says.'

'I don't believe you.'

'You'd better believe me because it's true.'

'What happened, John Joe?' Narrowing his eyes, he peers at me suspiciously. 'Did you ask him to take me?'

107

If I lie I can spare his feelings. If I tell the truth he may hate me.

Big breath.

'I did ask him, Roger. Because I'd be very unhappy to go without you.'

Nora Connolly's girls have rolled bandages for the mock battle. Everything must be just as it would in a real fight. I want to be a stretcher bearer, but that task will go to four of the older boys. The rest of us will serve as messengers. The stretcher bearers have stretchers and a First Aid box, and the Volunteers have weapons. Everyone has some sort of military equipment except the messengers. We only have our legs. It isn't fair – but Willie assures me it's the most important assignment of all. 'Good communication between officers is vital, John Joe. Without it an army is helpless.'

Following Mass on Easter morning, Madame and a friend of hers bring their motor cars to St Enda's to transport the Fianna to the mountains. The Volunteers are forming up elsewhere and will make the journey on foot. It isn't that far, we've done it lots of times.

Personally I think we should be allowed to march with them.

No one has said anything about bringing rations this time. But Roger – one can always count on Roger – sneaks down to the kitchen before we leave and loads his pockets with 'provisions'. Then we set off. There is great singing in both cars and a lot of horseplay. High spirits are the order of the day!

Carpeted with bracken and heather, the Dublin mountains are lovely in the spring. We turn off the main road into a narrow, rutted track, jolt along for a while, then make another turn into an even narrower track which is partially overgrown with briars. Thorns scrape along the sides of the cars. At last we come to a stop on a steep hillside studded with rock outcroppings.

'Are you sure this is the right place?' one of the older boys asks Madame. 'How are the troops going to find us up here?'

'They have a marked map,' she assures him.

The two automobiles go back the way they came. The briars close behind them. We're alone up here.

Roger begins emptying out his pockets. The stretcher bearers produce a flask of tea and a bag of biscuits. We sample everything, planning to save the rest for later. Then we scout the area as we've been taught in our drills. This is awfully rough ground. A lot of my time is spent helping Roger haul himself up some steep slope or other. I'm beginning to regret that I insisted he come along.

After what seems like hours, there is a noise like a

herd of cows crashing through the undergrowth.

The Volunteers have arrived!

'About time too,' says Roger, mopping the perspiration off his face.

The officers divide the men into two 'armies' to stage a mock attack and withdrawal. One group will hold a large rock outcropping while the others attempt to capture it. It's quite straightforward. We've done the same exercise in our own manoeuvres.

From the beginning, however, there is confusion. The new Volunteers are certainly eager, but it's like trying to herd cats. Orders are misunderstood or, worse yet, ignored. Some fellows don't seem to know their right from their left. Others wander off into the bracken and get lost. One man falls down and breaks his ankle, which gives the stretcher bearers something to do. They carry him down the mountain to a meadow where the women are waiting with their parked cars, and Madame's friend drives him back to Dublin and a doctor.

In the finish-up, there is no danger of Roger being unable to cope. The only Fianna who see service are the stretcher bearers. The rest of us spend our time trying to keep out of the way of the Volunteers as they blunder back and forth across the mountainside. Their officers make valiant attempts to establish order, but I don't envy them.

After a while Roger and I climb up onto a big rock and simply sit there watching. Unfortunately, by this stage he has eaten all there is to eat and there's none left for me.

At the end of the afternoon everyone is in a temper. The Volunteers have a long march back. The manoeuvre appears to have gone unnoticed by the authorities, so the older Fianna boys are allowed to go with them. The rest of us have another automobile ride. Mr Pearse is protecting us – wrapping us in cotton wool – more than I would like.

At least we're not as crowded in the cars as we were on the journey out.

Tonight in the dormitory everyone is talking about the exercise in the mountains. The boys who did not go are eager to hear all the details. I don't want to discuss it. But Roger is willing. He does puff up the story a bit and make it sound much more thrilling than it was, but maybe that's the way he remembers it.

I mostly remember being bored. Is that what a real war is like, I wonder?

I'm anxious about the coming summer. There has been no word from my father. Will he want me at home? Or can I stay here? St Enda's is not really equipped to keep students through the summer, and it would be unfair to ask.

But oh please dear sweet Mary and St Joseph, don't send me home.

Something terrible has happened! On the seventh of May a big ocean liner called the *Lusitania* was torpedoed by the Germans off the southern coast of Ireland. We've just heard the news. Hundreds of bodies are washing onto the beaches. There are pictures in the newspapers. At first I look at them as eagerly as the other boys, but now I can't bear to see them any more. It's too much to take in.

The newspapers predict that America, which has been neutral until now, will enter the Great War because of the *Lusitania*.

Looking at the big map of the world, I can see how tiny Ireland is in comparison with Europe on one side and America on the other. If the Germans invade England we will be the next step.

We should not have to suffer for the quarrels of the big nations. We need to be independent of the United Kingdom.

Summer is rushing toward us and everyone seems to assume that I will go home like the other students. The Ardmháistir looks very preoccupied these days. I feel guilty about bringing my small problem to him, but it's very big to me.

He is sitting behind his desk as usual, with a stack of

books and a huge pile of papers in front of him.

'Please, sir, have you heard anything from my father about the summer holidays?'

'What do you mean, John Joe?'

All my life I have been taught that children owe their parents total obedience and total loyalty. Sometimes that means keeping quiet about awful things. I must be very wicked to think of rebelling against my father, but I cannot face the thought of spending months in that house. I'm not a coward, it's just …

Screwing up my courage, I tell Mr Pearse. 'I don't want to go home, sir. You don't know what it's like.'

He gives me one of those long, quiet, measuring looks of his. Then he stands up and comes around to my side of the desk. He sits down in a chair which puts his face on a level with my own. In a calm voice he says, 'Perhaps you had best tell me what it's like, John Joe.'

It takes a long time. I start with little things, but then the bigger things come rushing to the surface. Twilight is gathering in the Ardmháistir's office and still I'm talking and still he's listening. The last and worst comes at the end.

Now I remember! Like some horrible nightmare that has pursued me into the daytime, I remember. And it's all happening again. Me cowering against the wall – I

must have been no more than three or four years old –
and my little mother standing in front of me, shielding
me with her body. I have committed some offence like
wetting my bed and my father is determined to punish
me severely. 'Over my dead body, Bertie!' Mam shouts
at him. It is the most defiant act I've ever seen. She is a
heroine, my mother.

He doubles his fist and clubs her to the floor.

CHAPTER ELEVEN

SUMMER 1915

The Ardmháistir showed me the letter he wrote to my father. It said in part, 'Your son is an exceptional young man. He is intelligent, honest, and has a fine character. You must be proud of him.

'We at St Enda's are proud of him too. That is why we should like to offer him a place here at the school during the summer. Our staff is much reduced during the holiday months and John Joe would be a welcome addition. My mother tells me he has been a great help to her in the past, and I am eager to make things as easy as possible for her now.

'If you will give your permission for your son to stay here we shall be most grateful. We are not in a position to offer him a regular salary, but shall pay him in kind. He will receive additional tutoring to enhance his education and prepare him to take a foremost place in a free society.

'As you must appreciate, since you entrusted the boy to us, we disagree with an educational system which prepares young people to be manageable slaves. The students of St Enda's are taught those noble and goodly things that will make them strong and proud and valiant. I believe John Joe will be an outstanding example of the success of our methods, and a great credit to you.'

I looked up from the letter in amazement. 'I don't see how my father can argue with that,' I told Mr Pearse. 'Yet everything you said is true.'

'Of course it is, John Joe. Except, perhaps, that part about your father being proud of you. But he *should* be, which is the point.'

How I would love to be a fly on the wall when my father read the letter. I shall never know what he said or how he felt – but by return of post he gave his permission.

If only I knew how to use words as well as Mr Pearse does. At least I have the whole summer to learn!

The St Enda's Fianna company will continue to drill here through the summer, so I shall be seeing my classmates on a regular basis. In addition, the Fianna girls will come out here to practice being auxiliaries.

Knowing Madame, I wonder she doesn't give them all guns and teach them how to shoot. Perhaps she will.

This summer I'll be able to tend my vegetable plot right through the season, instead of leaving it up to Michael MacRory. Each of us boys is responsible for his own little bit of soil and we get to choose what we want to grow. Last year I raised a crop of runner beans, the only vegetable I really like aside from potatoes. But I planted too many and we had to eat them almost every day.

I'm not as fond of runner beans any more.

This year I'm growing Brussels sprouts. I'm not sure why, unless it's because I don't like them very much. Maybe if I get to know them better I will. They do look like a great cluster of flowers when they're growing, so at least they are pretty.

From the moment I knew I would be staying at St Enda's, I felt as if a big black cloud had lifted off me. There is still a tiny little piece of it left, though. Next year is 1916 and it will have a summer, too. Sooner or later I shall have to face my father.

I don't want to think about that.

Maybe something will happen in the meantime and I won't have to go home next year either. Maybe I will stay right here at St Enda's and finish my education and become a teacher and teach here and my life will go on and on in this wonderful place.

The summer is flying by. Willie and his sister Margaret are helping me with my studies, and I am helping Mrs Pearse with her work. We spend every Monday together in the wash-house, which has a big copper for boiling the laundry in, wooden tubs for rinsing, and a mangle. The whole place smells of Sunlight Soap and Red Robin Starch. The Pearse brothers always have their collars and cuffs starched.

If it is not raining, the washing is hung to dry on the clotheslines that run from the wash-house to the wall by the grape arbour. I know I'm getting taller because I can peg the wet sheets onto the highest lines. Last year I could not. When I take them down again the sheets smell wonderfully fresh, like the wind off the sea. If no one is looking I bury my nose in them and take a deep breath.

Mr Pearse is not here very much these days. He is busy organising plans for the uprising. It's a privilege to know what is, after all, a very big secret. He can trust me not to tell anyone. Sometimes at night I lie in bed and hug myself in excitement. I wish I were just a few years older, though. I wish the uprising could wait until I'm old enough to be a Volunteer.

The Fianna will have a part to play, however. In our

drills this summer we are practising tunnelling and transporting supplies and cleaning weapons. The older boys even practice shooting with live ammunition, but I'm not allowed to yet. I know I would be a crack shot if they only gave me the chance. I have very keen eyes.

One week Roger does not show up for Fianna drill. Con Colbert explains to the rest of us, 'Roger has received bad news, I'm afraid. His brother Donald has been killed in France. His body is on its way home for burial.'

Poor Roger! I remember how I felt when Mam died, it's the most awful, alone sort of feeling. There is nothing I can do that would make things any easier for my friend. We have a Mass said for Donald, and I ask Willie to help me make a sympathy card to send to Roger.

'What would you like to paint on the front of it, John Joe?'

That's a hard question. What is the symbol for sympathy? At last I decide on an Easter lily because of the Resurrection. Roger's a Protestant but they believe in the Resurrection just the same as we do.

I still don't know what to write inside the card.

'What do you think?' I ask Willie.

'What do you feel?'

'Well, I'm terribly sorry about Donald.'

'There's your answer, John Joe. You should always say what's in your heart. If it's honest it need not be fancy. That's what Pat does; he always says what's in his heart.'

On the first of August there will be another funeral in Dublin. Jeremiah O'Donovan Rossa, who was one of the greatest of the Fenians, died in New York in June. His body has been sent home for burial in Glasnevin Cemetery. Wearing dress uniform, the Fianna will march in the funeral procession. Mr Pearse will give the graveside oration.

The St Enda's Fianna are summoned to the school for a special drill beforehand. Even Roger attends. He is wearing a black armband, as I did for my mother. There is something strange about those mourning bands. They are only a little strip of cloth, yet when you have one on you are conscious of it all the time. It's like a weight dragging at your arm.

Roger looks pale and hollow-eyed and does not ask if there will be refreshments afterward. Otherwise he seems normal enough – until one of the older boys says something about the war.

'The war!' cries Roger. 'The war took my brother and blew him to bits and sent him home in a box with the lid nailed down. Don't talk to me about the war!'

Then he bursts into tears.

I'm his best friend but I don't know what to do.

Unfortunately Mr Pearse is not with us on the playing

field, he is in his office writing the oration. But Mrs Pearse has come to watch us, and she comes hurrying over to gather Roger into her arms. Her face looks as stricken as his. 'You poor boy, you poor boy,' she murmurs as she strokes his hair. 'And your poor mother too. She is in my prayers. It is such a terrible thing to lose a child.'

Roger pulls away with blazing eyes. 'She didn't lose him, they took him away from her and killed him!' Turning to me, he cries, 'Donald died for King George!'

I have never seen such bitterness on any face.

The Irish soldiers being slaughtered on the Western Front in the name of the king are honoured by people here as heroes. That is right and proper, because there is no doubt they were brave men. But Roger is not thinking about his brother's heroism, only about the waste of his life. I understand how he feels. Donald was young and strong and now he is dead and cold, sacrificed for a cause that was not his.

O'Donovan Rossa spent his life in the struggle for Ireland's freedom.

On the day before the funeral, his embalmed body lies in state in City Hall. The Pearses take me into the city with them to pay respects. Uniformed members of the Volunteers serve as a guard of honour around the coffin, which is standing on trestles. The lid is open.

That means we shall get to see him. The only other dead person I've ever seen was Mam.

It won't be as bad this time.

Following Margaret Pearse, I join the queue of people filing past the coffin. Many are carrying rosaries. Quite a few are weeping. Did they know him when he was alive? I wish I had. If it were not for Mr Pearse I would know nothing about O'Donovan Rossa's gallant struggle, and that of the other Fenians, to break Ireland's chains.

At last I look down at the pale face on the satin pillow. His gaunt features are very noble. Willie Pearse could sculpt that face. Perhaps one day he will. I expect there will be magnificent statues by William Pearse in museums all over Ireland in years to come. I shall go to see them and tell the admiring crowd, 'I knew him, you know. Willie Pearse was a friend of mine.'

Ned Halloran is one of the members of the guard of honour standing at the four corners of the coffin. When no one is looking he gives me the tiniest wink. At least I think he does. He looks so stern and grown-up it's hard to tell. He has crossed an invisible line and become a man. When will I cross that line? I wonder. Will I know it when it comes?

August first is Lughnasa, the ancient Celtic festival of the sun. But we won't see much of the sun today. By the time the funeral procession forms up outside City Hall, a bank of heavy cloud is building in the north. In turn, the Irish Volunteers, the Citizen Army, the Fianna, Cumann na mBan, the Irish Girl Guides, the National Foresters, and the Hibernian hurling teams all take their place in the long procession.

With the exception of their officers, most of the Volunteers still do not have uniforms. James Connolly has got funding from somewhere so the Citizen Army is sporting a new dark green uniform. I think the Fianna are better drilled than either organisation, though I must admit they are improving. But we're the only ones who manage to march in step.

Priests and labour union officers and members of the literary community join the procession too. There is no representative from the government, however. The British government that rules Ireland.

I don't think O'Donovan Rossa would want them anyway.

Accompanied by a sombre rattle of drums, he sets out on his final journey.

A large crowd has turned out to line the streets on the way to Glasnevin Cemetery. The men remove their hats as the coffin passes by, and the women throw paper flowers since there are few real ones to be had at this time of year.

When we reach Glasnevin the Dublin Metropolitan Police are waiting for us. They are all very tall men, wearing dark blue uniforms and metal helmets with spikes on top. They are supposed to look intimidating, and they do. As the procession starts through the gates the police do not try to stop it, but I see several of them with notebooks out, taking down names.

A crowd of civilians has also been waiting for us outside the cemetery. As the Fianna approach the gates a woman exclaims, 'Look at those dear little lads in their costumes!'

My face flames. We are *not* 'dear little lads'. We are warriors of Ireland! I throw my head back and march forward like the soldier I am.

Joe Plunkett is in charge of the arrangements at Glasnevin today. He has everything well organised. Inside the cemetery gates two of the youngest Fianna are handing out beautifully printed programmes and pasteboard passes to the graveside, where a crowd is already waiting. Older members of the Fianna are setting up camp chairs for women and old people.

O'Donovan Rossa will not be alone in his final sleep. On every side lie the graves of other Fenians. Some have rosary beads draped over the headstones. The oldest stones are settling back into the earth, the way I snuggle back into my quilt on a cold night.

This is a very solemn place. Very peaceful. But the skies are overcast and there is a sort of tingling in the air. Maybe a storm is coming.

Wearing the uniform of a Commandant of the Volunteers, Padraic Pearse steps forward. He is taller than most of the men around him. He takes a folded piece of paper from the pocket of his tunic, then removes his peaked cap and tucks it under his arm before beginning the graveside oration.

He speaks slowly, in a deep, strong voice. From his first words, the large crowd is spellbound. No one coughs or even rustles a programme. They listen to every word as if they had never heard such words before. And perhaps they have not. The Ardmháistir is speaking of splendour and pride and strength as *Irish* qualities.

'Our foes are strong, and wise, and wary,' he says, 'but they cannot undo the miracles of God, Who ripens in the hearts of young men the seeds sown by the young men of a former generation.'

Young men. Like me.

The final words of Padraic Pearse's speech carve themselves on my heart.

'I hold it a Christian thing, as O'Donovan Rossa held it, to hate evil, to hate untruth, to hate oppression, and hating them, to strive to overthrow them.

'Life springs from death, and from the graves of patriot men spring live nations. The defenders of this realm have worked well in secret and in the open. They think they have pacified Ireland. They think that they have purchased half of us, and intimidated the other half.'

Mr Pearse pauses; takes a deep breath. Raising his chin, he looks out across the sea of headstones. I would swear there is a faint smile on his lips.

'They think that they have provided against everything; but the fools, the fools, the fools! They have left us our Fenian dead, and while Ireland holds these graves, Ireland unfree shall never be at peace!'

CHAPTER TWELVE

AUTUMN 1915

After the Ardmháistir's speech there is absolute silence. Then a party of Volunteers step forward and fire a volley over the grave. How the crack of gunfire echoes!

The Fianna march in a body to the Botanic Gardens to be collected by their families – or in my case, a motor car which will take myself and the Pearse women out to Rathfarnham.

As we walk along Roger is very quiet. He does not look around, but only down at his feet. When he sees his parents looking for him he slouches off to join them without even saying goodbye.

Mrs Pearse and her daughters are waiting for me in a

taxicab parked at the kerb outside the Gardens. The Pearses do not own a motorcar; I suppose all their money goes into the school. Willie and even the Ardmháistir usually travel by bicycle.

When I sit into the taxicab Mrs Pearse says, 'I have never heard Pat speak so well, have you?'

Before I can reply, Mary Brigid clasps her hands together and cries, 'Oh was he not splendid? Was he not magnificent?'

Margaret Pearse frowns at her sister. 'You're exaggerating again, Mary Brigid,' she says sternly. 'Please make an effort to control yourself.' She sounds annoyed. She always sounds annoyed when she speaks to Mary Brigid.

They are nothing alike. Margaret Pearse looks like the spinster she is, with her hair scraped back into a knot and gold-rimmed spectacles perched on the end of her nose. Mary Brigid is smaller, softer. She has a pretty face and a fluttery manner, like a bird about to take wing. In fact she has taken wing. She is no longer living at the Hermitage, but has rented a little house in the village of Rathfarnham. I don't know if it was her idea or not. I suspect the family finally found her too difficult to live with and suggested she would be happier elsewhere.

But I secretly agree with Mary Brigid about her

brother's speech. When you hear something as grand as that, it's easy to be swept away.

Maybe when I grow up I shall be an orator.

Roger returns to school for the autumn term with the other students. He is still moody, not like his old self at all.

At St Enda's we are taught to pay attention to every living thing and try to understand how others feel. I've never done that before, but now I cannot help doing it. I suspect Roger is torn between loyalty to his brothers, which includes the cause they serve, and a growing feeling of loyalty to the land of his birth. I'm glad I don't have that problem.

In September twelve hundred Irish Volunteers march openly through Dublin carrying Howth rifles. That same month, the women of Cumann na mBan stage their first parade in their new uniforms. Meanwhile the companies of the Fianna are drilling like veterans all around the city. The Irish Girl Guides are drilling too, just like Cumann na mBan and the Citizen Army. It's very exciting, so many ordinary men and women, boys and girls, all of us saying to the King of England, 'We don't want to fight in your war. We want our own country back.'

But will he listen? I don't think so. He is too busy quarrelling with his cousins. I read in the newspapers that Czar Nicholas has now taken personal command of the Russian army. I wonder if King George will do the same. Those two sovereigns should meet one another on the battlefield and have a battle of champions, just the two of them, the way it was done in Ireland at the time of the Fianna. Then no one else – like Roger's brother – would have to die. And when it is over they can exchange gifts and be friends again, as Roger and I did.

It seems very simple to me. It's the adults who make things complicated.

My friend Roger never misses a drill. Sometimes he seems to enjoy them. Other times one can see his heart isn't in it. He still thinks he's supposed to be British. If we really do have an uprising, I wonder how many other people in Ireland will feel the way he does?

It takes a lot of courage to break free. Many Irish people don't seem to care if they are dominated by a foreign power. My father's like that. The British government employs him so he's content to have them here. He simply passes the domination on to anyone who's weaker than he is.

Being at St Enda's has given me a chance to look at things in a whole new way. After the uprising, when Ireland is free, maybe there will be schools like this all over the country, and our people can learn what an ancient and glorious heritage we have. Then they will be proud to be Irish instead of trying to be English.

Maybe I'll be a teacher in one of those schools.

After O'Donovan Rossa's funeral Mr Pearse is called away to more meetings than ever. There is more marching, too, by both the Volunteers and the Citizen Army. I wonder why they don't join up and do everything together?

I'll ask Willie. He has become like the big brother I wish I had. I guess I feel about him the way he feels about the Ardmháistir.

My question makes him laugh. 'You have a good head on you, John Joe, but it's the old Irish story. Rivalry instead of cooperation. The leaders of the Volunteers are intellectuals like my brother and Tom Mac-Donagh and Joe Plunkett. The Citizen Army was created by the leaders of the labour unions and is mainly working class. Each corps has its own command structure and its own way of doing things. Also, the two groups have differing visions for Ireland.'

'What do you mean?'

'Pat and his friends want an independent Irish Republic. James Connolly is a socialist. He and his followers are interested in creating a socialist state.'

'Cannot Ireland be both?'

Willie nods. 'Possibly. But neither group can achieve what it wants unless Ireland is free. Britain will never willingly allow Ireland to become an independent republic because that would set a bad example. Other conquered colonial possessions might demand their freedom too.

'The Empire is built on capitalism, so Britain will not allow Ireland to go socialist, either. Socialism means giving working men equal rights with industrialists and that's against everything the Empire stands for.'

'Do you think we can ever win our freedom, Willie?'

'The Americans did,' he points out.

'Will they help us?' To show him that I know quite a lot already, I ask, 'Is the Irish Republican Brotherhood an American organisation?'

Willie looks startled. 'How do you know about the IRB?'

'I once overheard you and the Ardmháistir talking about it. You were in his office and the door was open.'

'You never should have heard that!'

'I've never mentioned it to anyone else and I never will,' I assure him. 'But just what is the IRB, Willie?'

'You know about the Fenian Brotherhood which was founded in New York in 1848, and to which O'Donovan Rossa belonged. Well, the Irish Republican Brotherhood was founded in Dublin ten years later. Together they form an underground movement whose sole purpose is, and always has been, to set Ireland free. The IRB is secretly funding the Volunteers, using money raised in America. We're hoping for aid from the Germans, too, in the form of weapons.'

It is my turn to be startled. 'I thought we were at war with Germany!'

'Ireland has never been at war with Germany, John Joe. The Germans have done us no harm. Britain, which has been our enemy and oppressor for centuries, *is* at war with Germany – and the enemy of our enemy is our friend.'

Imagine that! Nations far across the sea reaching out their hands to help Ireland! On the world map we are so small, yet we have powerful friends.

At least I hope we do. As I recall from my Irish history studies, we thought the French were our friends and would help us, but in 1798 they let Wolfe Tone down badly.

Can we trust anyone but ourselves?

There is a small nationalist political party here which calls itself Sinn Féin: Ourselves Alone. Sinn Féin was founded by a man called Arthur Griffith.

The Irish Parliamentary Party is much larger. They seem content to work within the system we have. Their leader, John Redmond, has urged the Irish Volunteers to enlist in the British Army. He promises that Britain will reward them by giving us Home Rule when the war is over.

Eoin MacNeill, who is President and Chief-of-Staff of the Volunteers, disagrees. He says Home Rule is a cheque the British will continually post-date. Professor MacNeill teaches early Irish history at University College Dublin and is a very intelligent man.

Besides, even if we did get Home Rule we still would not be independent of Britain. I think independence is terribly important. It's like growing up; being in charge of your own life.

Before I came to St Enda's I knew nothing about politics. Now I see that politics is like a giant, invisible spider web all around us. According to the Ardmháistir politics affects every part of our lives – how we live, what we earn, even what our old age will be like. When I was a child I never thought about such things.

But I'm about to be a man.

If I try to talk about politics with Roger, he gets that stubborn look he gets sometimes. 'Nothing to do with me,' he says.

I guess Roger's not ready to be a man yet.

There are lots of secrets now: secret meetings, secret plans, secret military manoeuvres late at night. St Enda's is right at the heart of everything – at least the Ardmháistir is. Professor MacNeill may be Chief-of-Staff, but Mr

Pearse has a lot of influence in the Volunteers. He is Director of Organisation and also part of a secret Provisional Committee within the Volunteer Corps.

The Committee consists of members of the Irish Republican Brotherhood. Professor MacNeill does not belong.

I'm not supposed to know this. But when I went to the Ardmháistir's office this afternoon, looking for Willie, I saw a packet of papers on Mr Pearse's desk with a slip of paper on top. On the paper is written 'Faoi rún', which means 'In confidence' in English.

No one was in the office. A person who was not meant to see those papers could have walked in and read them, and I was sure Mr Pearse would not like that. So I carefully put them away in the top drawer of his desk – after I took a quick look through them myself.

I shall never tell a soul what those papers contain; not ever. But I'm thankful I can read Irish now.

The plans for the uprising are much farther along than I thought. After New Year's there will be a meeting to set the actual date. Companies of Volunteers down the country are eagerly awaiting more weapons. Once those arrive they will be ready to march. Auxiliary organisations such as Cumann na mBan are waiting to support the men in the field with first aid and a constant flow of supplies. The Fianna, too, will play a strategic part.

Strategic means we boys are absolutely necessary to the success of the uprising!

CHAPTER THIRTEEN

WINTER 1915

I wish I could tell someone what I know, but I can't. A secret is not a secret if you tell. Besides, the Pearses trust me and I will never betray their trust.

With Christmas approaching, I am growing anxious. It is too much to hope that my father has forgotten about me. This year surely he will demand I come home, and if he does, Mr Pearse will have to let me go.

Roger is going to leave the school a few days early to spend more time with his family. 'The holidays will be awful,' he moans, 'with James still at the front and Donald ...' He can't finish the sentence.

'At least you have both your parents,' I say consolingly. For a wild moment I'm tempted to ask if I can go home with him. But how could I explain? I have not told anyone but the Ardmháistir about the things my father does, and I never shall. The years of beatings and the fear that never goes away – those are my secrets.

Yet in spite of them, I can never betray my father.

Sometimes I wonder if all fathers are like mine. Maybe they are. And their children never tell.

To my relief, my father has asked that I be kept at the school for the holidays. Mrs Pearse just gave me the news. She seems genuinely puzzled, both by the request and my cheerfulness about it.

The explanation I give her is, partly, the truth. 'My father works in Dublin Castle and they're terribly busy right now. There is no one at home to mind me, so I'm happy enough to stay here if it will make things easier for him.'

She gives me a little hug. 'You are a brave and under-standing lad, John Joe. But I do think the man could make arrangements to spend at least a few days with you. Even the Castle shuts down for Christmas.'

Actually that's not true. There is a possibility that con-scription will be announced within a matter of weeks, and the lights are burning late in government offices. If conscription does go through English men will be shipped off to the Great War whether they want to go or not. Can Ireland be far behind?

Mary Brigid comes home to the Hermitage for the holidays and every evening we are treated to a harp concert in the family dining room. Sometimes I close my eyes and pretend it's *my* family dining room, with my mother and my brothers and sisters around me.

Later I lie in my bed and wonder how my father is, and what he's doing. Is he lonely? Should I not be with him?

Part of me feels awfully guilty.

To my surprise, one afternoon Aunt Nell comes out to the school to spend a few hours with me. She has tea with us and makes polite conversation with Mrs Pearse. 'I would take John Joe home with me for the holidays,' she says, 'but I have just a wee little cottage and there's no room for an active boy.'

'I understand completely,' says Mrs Pearse. But I know her, she's just being agreeable. She could not really understand anyone who did not want to have a boy in their house. Her entire family loves children. They have dedicated their lives to us.

Aunt Nell is making an effort, however. She gives me a Christmas present – a box of socks – and another gift which she says is from my father. 'Bertie's after sending you half a crown,' she tells me, 'for pocket money.'

My father would not give me half a crown if his life depended on it. I suspect it came from her own purse.

Sometimes I really am fond of my aunt. She hides it well, but I think she has a good heart.

On *Nollaig na mBan,* the sixth of January, the House of Commons votes overwhelmingly for conscription. Single men will be called up first, but the newspapers say married men may go soon. The slaughter at the front is enormous and calls for more and more bodies.

We shall be next. The generals have always put the Irish in the front lines to spare English lives.

Meanwhile the number of Irish men volunteering for the British army has slowed to a trickle. Thousands are drilling with the Volunteers instead. Recruiting meetings are held in the towns and villages – Mr Pearse goes to a lot of those – and country roads feel the thud of marching feet.

We cheer them when they come past St Enda's.

More of the Volunteers have uniforms now. Those who don't, wear Sam Browne belts and soft hats to identify them as members of Ireland's own army. They may be poorly equipped and short of almost everything, but there is no doubting their courage. The Dublin Brigade continues to carry firearms openly. The police watch but make no effort to stop them. I don't think the government knows what to do about the situation. They were severely criticised for the disaster on Bachelor's Walk and they are preoccupied with the

Great War. Maybe they hope the nationalist movement will just go away.

It won't.

I wonder what my father, secure behind the walls of Dublin Castle, makes of all this. He has shown no interest in me since I'm off his hands, but surely he cannot be unaware of the Ardmháistir's republican connections. At some stage will he demand that I resign from the Fianna and leave St Enda's?

Let him. If he does, I shall rebel openly. Even run away if I must. Maybe one of Mr Pearse's friends in the IRB would hide me.

Yesterday the Dublin Brigade carried out a sham attack on the post office! It was planned with the greatest secrecy and carried out quietly; neither the Citizen Army nor the Fianna took part. However we've been promised that we shall share the action on St Patrick's Day, when military reviews will be held all across the country.

We're going to shake our fists at King George.

Dublin Castle is concerned about the growing tide of Irish nationalism. Some prominent activists have been arrested and charged with 'sedition', which means urging rebellion. They are being held in prison but so far none have stood trial.

It's important that the government has no idea of our

real strength. There was a small item in one of the newspapers this morning, to the effect that there are only nine hundred 'outlawed' rifles in the hands of the Dublin Volunteers, and less than five thousand in the whole country.

Willie says the Castle is guilty of underestimating. 'That's what Pat wants them to do, John Joe. It means we shall have the element of surprise with us.'

'How many weapons do we really have, then?'

Willie frowns. 'That's not my department, but I'm certain we have more than the Castle claims. Plus we're expecting tens of thousands more. We'll need them; when the time comes as many as a hundred thousand men may be standing with us. More than enough to win our freedom.'

I hope those weapons from Germany arrive soon.

Willie has told me a very big secret. The IRB has set the date for the uprising as Easter Sunday, the twenty-third of April.

'Don't breathe a word of this, John Joe,' he warns me. 'You are in a very privileged position because you've almost become part of the family here. Even Eoin MacNeill does not know a date's been set.'

'Why not? Isn't he the chief-of-staff of the Volunteers?'

'He is. But the professor insists the corps must be

used only as a defensive force. He will not allow them to go on the offensive.'

'How can we win our independence by fighting defensively? That doesn't make sense.'

'Pat agrees with you,' says Willie. 'That's why the arrangements he and the others are making must be kept secret.'

A number of sealed crates have arrived and been stored in the wash-house, to Mrs Pearse's annoyance. The lights burn all night in the Ardmháistir's office, where he is writing articles and pamphlets to prepare the country for the uprising.

During the day he has a steady stream of callers, including Joe Plunkett, who dresses in a flowing cape like an actor and wears a lot of jewellery, and a handsome young man with a limp, Seán MacDermott, who travels all around Ireland on a bicycle as an organiser for the Volunteers.

Another visitor is a frail old man called Tom Clarke who owns a tobacconist shop in Dublin. He looks quite harmless, he's as thin as a rake and wears strong spectacles. Yet Willie tells me Mr Clarke spent years in a British prison and is a hero of the republican movement. I would love to talk to him. I've never known anyone who's been in prison. The nearest I came was Jim Larkin's son.

There is an air of tense anticipation at St Enda's. Thanks to the increase in preparations, I'm not the only boy who knows what's going on. Most of the Fianna have a good idea, especially the officers. I may be the only one who is aware that Professor MacNeill is being kept in the dark, though.

Willie tells me, with tremendous pride, that there has been a secret meeting of the IRB Military Council and Mr Pearse as been appointed Commander-in-Chief. When the uprising begins our own Ardmháistir will be in charge.

Yet life goes on at the school. We sit in our class-rooms and study our textbooks and, about the middle of every afternoon, get a little bored and sleepy and wish we were doing something else.

Roll on, April!

One Saturday morning Roger and I go down to Emmet's Fort for a game of pirates. To our surprise we find four of the Girl Guides there, including Marcella. This time she has a bright red ribbon in her hair. I don't know if I could ride around on a horse wearing a red ribbon on my arm. Besides, I notice that she has skinned knees. I don't think Fair Ladies are supposed to have skinned knees.

'This is our place,' Roger growls at the girls, 'and you don't belong here.'

'We have just as much right to be here as you do,' Marcella says with her fists on her hips. She's only half his size but one can tell she won't back down.

'What are you doing here anyway?'

'We came out with Miss Connolly and her father. They brought us along for the drive.'

So James Connolly is paying a call on Mr Pearse!

We don't dare throw the girls out. Mr Pearse is very strict about always treating women with courtesy; even girls with skinned knees. Suddenly it seems to me that playing pirates is childish. When I suggest we play rebellion instead, the others enthusiastically agree.

I am Padraic Pearse and Roger is James Connolly. The girls comprise the Volunteers and the Citizen Army. We search the woods for dead branches the size of rifles, then the girls march up and down with their weapons on their shoulders while Roger and I bark out orders.

The woodland is Dublin. The enemy is hiding among the buildings – that's the trees. Every shadow could conceal lurking death. Roger and I plan tactics for our fearless troops. The girls do some amazingly clever things on their own, like camouflaging themselves with laurel branches threaded through their jumpers. It's great fun for a while – until Marcella rebels. 'I think it's our turn to give orders now,' she tells me.

'But you're girls!'

'Countess Markievicz gives orders and she's an officer in the Citizen Army.'

'That's different.' I resent her using Madame to prove her point. Madame is special.

'If we can't have our turn,' says Marcella – with her fists on her hips again – 'we won't play. You'll just have to recruit your old army from somewhere else.'

Turning on her heel, she marches away with her back as straight as a soldier's and laurel twigs still caught in her jumper. After a moment's hesitation her friends follow her.

Roger looks at me. 'Now see what you've done.'

'It wasn't my fault.' At least I don't think it was. How could things go sour so fast?

Roger and I skip stones across the pond for a while, then some of the other boys come along and we play rebellion again. But it isn't the same.

CHAPTER FOURTEEN

MARCH 1916

O n St Patrick's Day there is a demonstration of nationalist feeling all across the country, with speeches and banners and parades. In Dublin a reviewing stand has been built on College Green, where Professor MacNeill will take the salute of the Dublin Brigade of Irish Volunteers.

Since eleven in the morning the battalions have been gathering at designated churches. They converge on Stephen's Green, where they go through some manoeuvres while a number of curious people watch. To anyone who has seen photographs of a regular army the Volunteers don't look very professional. In age they run from old men down to mere boys who have never yet shaved, and some of their weapons are laughable. Those who did not get Howth rifles make do with antique guns or shot-guns or even pikestaffs.

But they have their hearts in their eyes.

The Fianna join the parade in full uniform and feeling very proud. The oldest boys march in front; I am in the second rank. By next year I shall be big enough to march in the first rank. But everything may be very different next year.

Ireland may be free.

Ireland may be free!

I hug those words to my chest.

At Trinity a crowd of college students has gathered to watch the parade. Most of them are Protestant and members of the Ascendancy, so their sympathies are British. A few of them jeer at us or make mocking gestures, but for the most part they just watch. Perhaps they are surprised by our numbers.

Eoin MacNeill on the reviewing stand wears rimless spectacles and looks very like a professor. Not like a warrior, though. I think the Provisional Committee is right to keep its plans from him. In brilliant spring sunshine he is wearing an overcoat all buttoned up and a thick muffler wrapped twice around. MacNeill is obviously a cautious man. There is no place for cautious men in a revolution. When we were studying the life of

Wolfe Tone Mr Pearse told us, 'He hoped for the best and dared the worst.'

I shall hope for the best. I cannot imagine what 'the worst' might be, but we will know soon enough. It is only six weeks until Easter.

Once again the police are on duty to observe the movements of the Volunteers. And once again I see them taking down names. They don't approach any of the Fianna, of course. They think we are harmless. Like Tom Clarke.

I feel like thumbing my nose at the police.

When the review is over we disband, and most of the Fianna from St Enda's go back to the school. A few of the older boys decide to stay in Dublin for a while and return to Rathfarnham later by tram. I don't think there is much to do in town. Because today is a holiday all the shops are closed.

But the feast day of Ireland's patron saint is no holiday as far as the British are concerned. Dublin Castle is not closed. At the seat of government, today is just another Friday.

From Trinity to the Castle is only a short walk.

I've never visited my father at work. When I suddenly appear in my uniform he will see that I am almost a man, and not afraid of him any more.

I set out briskly for the Castle. When I reach the

fancy iron gates I slow my pace, then stop altogether. The guard on duty in the guard box gives me a curious look.

I almost, *almost,* ask for admittance. At the last moment my nerve fails me and I turn and go back the way I came. By the time I reach College Green I'm shaking. I've never been so angry with myself. I did not dare the worst.

Next time I shall.

On the day after St Patrick's there is an article in the paper which makes me laugh out loud, though I suppose it's not meant to be funny. Since the beginning of the Great War Britain has urged women to take up jobs outside the home so their menfolk will be free to fight. In Liverpool, women working at the dockyards have now quit their jobs because the men refuse to work with them.

I wonder if Marcella reads the newspapers?

The next weeks are spent in feverish activity. The Ardmháistir will not allow any of us to slacken our studies, but the Fianna drill every single afternoon, rain or sun. It's easy to see why we are necessary. We will serve as scouts and messengers and join the women in carrying ammunition to the men. I hope to be assigned to the stretcher-bearers. If there are any casualties during the uprising the stretcher-bearers will be sent for right away and get to see everything.

'You just want to see the blood, John Joe,' Roger accuses.

'Don't you?'

'Blood makes me sick to my stomach.'

'You're full of blood yourself, eejit!'

When he turns pale, I laugh.

Actually I don't think we're going to see any blood. Willie says there are tens of thousands of Volunteers down the country now, not to mention the Citizen Army and the other nationalist organisations. Because of the Great War the number of British soldiers garrisoned in Ireland is at an all-time low. My father has always said that the British are very sensible, much more so than the Irish. When they see how strong we are and how determined we are, they will do the sensible thing and give in.

At the very least they will allow us to have Home Rule.

In church on Ash Wednesday the priest scribes the cross on my forehead, saying, 'Remember man, thou art dust and to dust thou shalt return.'

Afterward Roger teases me about my ashes. 'I'll have to teach you a good Protestant poem, John Joe. "Ashes to ashes and dust to dust, if God won't have you the Devil must."'

So I hit him. Then he hits me. Only once each, though.

Good Friday is a sombre occasion at the school. Most of the boys have gone home for the holiday, of course. With the Pearse family, I keep the vigil and follow the Stations of the Cross. I'm trying hard to concentrate on the meaning of the day, on Christ's love for us and his great sacrifice, but my thoughts keep running ahead to Sunday. Not to Christ's resurrection but to Ireland's.

On Saturday morning, the St Enda's Fianna are summoned to a meeting at the school. Not a single boy fails to attend, though some have had to travel quite a distance. A silvery sea of bicycles lies at the edge of the playing field.

'I shall not be with you tomorrow,' Con Colbert tells us, 'because I have been chosen as bodyguard to the Commander-in-Chief.'

What an honour! Oh, if only the uprising could wait for two or three more years – *I* might be Padraic Pearse's bodyguard!

'The plan,' Con Colbert continues, 'is to seize a number of strategic locations throughout Dublin, including the General Post Office, which will become Headquarters because it's centrally located and the telegraph's on the top floor. As soon as we have control of communications we can prevent the authorities from sending to England for more troops.

'The nearby rural battalions, such as Thomas Ashe's men in North County Dublin, will join us in Dublin. Meanwhile the Volunteer brigades down the country will capture their local garrisons.'

'What about us, sir?' I ask eagerly.

'You boys have worked very hard to be ready, but by the order of the Commander-in-Chief only those of fifteen and over will be allowed in the contested areas on Sunday. The rest of you will be assigned to duties well away from any possible danger. Be assured that whatever you are asked to do will be very important.'

Fifteen and over. I've been growing as fast as I can and I'm as big as any fifteen-year-old boy. But my birthday will not be until October.

I'm too old to cry and too young to take part in the Easter Rising.

The most important thing that has ever happened in my entire life is going to happen without me.

I glance over at Roger, who is a month younger than I. One would expect him to be relieved. Poor pudgy Roger would not make a very fleet-footed messenger anyway. But he looks almost as disappointed as I am. 'I should have expected this,' he mutters, hanging his head. When the other boys choose up sides for games,

Roger is always the last one taken.

The older boys are given specific instructions for tomorrow. They will report to posts around the city and await further orders from the officers. The rest of us are to keep ourselves 'in readiness'.

I know what that means. We're to stay home and wait.

I'm not very good at waiting.

'I guess I won't see you tomorrow,' Roger tells me. He looks so downcast I feel sorry for him.

'Maybe you will. Maybe they'll send for us after all,' I say in an effort to cheer him up.

He only shakes his head.

Willie is at St Enda's this afternoon, working in his studio. There is no sign of the Ardmháistir. I suppose he is tending to last-minute details in the city. I wander around the house, feeling rather lost. The classrooms and study hall are empty. I am the sole inhabitant of the dormitory. It's funny how a place seems to echo when you know there are not many people around.

Mrs Pearse and Margaret would not mind if I sat in the parlour with them – they are doing some sewing – but I cannot sit still for very long, so there's no point. Instead I wander around the grounds. They are so beautiful. Everything has been arranged to make St Enda's a heaven for growing boys.

It's hard to imagine that a revolution is about to begin beyond the safety of these walls.

And I won't be there!

I have little appetite for tea when it is served. Willie eats nothing at all. After a short while he excuses himself and goes into the Ardmháistir's office. I can just barely hear the rumble of his voice; he's making telephone calls.

At last I take a book from the library and go up to bed. Maybe I can read myself to sleep.

The book is a collection of stories by Rudyard Kipling. They are exciting tales, full of wild animals and grand adventures. I'm almost able to forget about the Rising for a while. Just as my eyelids finally are growing heavy Willie enters the room. He has a strange expression on his face.

'I'm afraid something has gone wrong, John Joe.'

CHAPTER FIFTEEN

EASTER SUNDAY 1916

I sit up so quickly my book slides to the floor. Mr Pearse would not like that, he insists that we take very good care of books.

'What's wrong?' I want to know.

Willie sits down wearily on the next bed. 'Eoin Mac-Neill found out about our plans. He's issued an order countermanding Pat's orders.'

I don't understand. 'Can he do that? Mr Pearse is the Commander-in-Chief now, is he not?'

'He is – but no one told Professor MacNeill. We were afraid he might interfere and now he has. The story was in the late edition of the papers.'

'Do you mean the rising's been called off?' A tiny part

of me feels a sudden guilty pleasure. If the revolution is postponed until next Easter I'll be fifteen …

Willie says, 'We don't dare call it off, John Joe. We've learned that Dublin Castle has issued orders for the arrest of a hundred leading nationalists by the end of the week. If the Rising does not go ahead almost immediately, Pat and Tom and James Connolly and the others will be in prison. God knows what the British will do to them when they learn what's been planned, as they surely will. Our men might even be shot for treason. Pat surely would; he's been appointed President of the Provisional Irish Republic.'

President of the Republic. Our Ardmháistir.

'If we go ahead,' says Willie, 'we have the IRB behind us, and they are a force to be reckoned with. They won't slink away with their tails between their legs, the way Irish rebels have done in the past. We're in this fight to the finish now. Because MacNeill's countermand specifically states that the Volunteers are to stand down on Sunday, we are going to begin the Rising on Monday. Everything else will be just as before. In fact, there may be a slight advantage. The British troops stationed in Dublin will be out of the city, attending the races at Fairyhouse. It's an Easter Monday tradition with them.'

Easter Monday. We'll have our Easter Rising after all.

After Willie leaves the dormitory I lie sleepless in the dark. Once or twice I get out of bed to look out the window. The stars are very bright and very far away. Midnight has passed. It is Easter.

In the morning the entire Pearse family attends Mass together. The church positively reeks of lilies. I don't like the smell of lilies, they remind me too much of Mam's funeral.

From my place at the far end of the pew I occasionally sneak glances at the Ardmháistir. His face is very calm. He is the sort of man who, once he's made up his mind, ceases to worry. Whatever happens now he is committed.

And so am I.

The Easter Rising is not going to take place without me.

CHAPTER SIXTEEN

EASTER MONDAY 1916

On Monday morning Willie and Mr Pearse get early Mass. Then they are joined at the Hermitage by Con Colbert, Ned Halloran, and another St Enda's student called Des Ryan, who sometimes works as Mr Pearse's secretary. All five wear Volunteer uniforms and have bicycles.

Off to set Ireland free, on a bicycle.

Mrs Pearse and Margaret stand on the front steps to bid the little party goodbye. This is a family moment, so I hang back and watch from the doorway. The Ardmháistir bends down to allow his mother to kiss his cheek. She tells him, 'Now Pat, don't do anything rash.'

'No, Mother,' he replies quite solemnly.

As he is about to mount his bicycle he sees me and beckons me down to him. I am bareheaded, and he tousles my hair. My father never tousled my hair. 'Do not forget to pray for us,' Padraic Pearse says.

'I won't forget, sir.' I snap my best salute.

With a smile, he returns the salute. 'We hope for the best and dare the worst, John Joe.'

Then he is gone.

I stand on the gravel waving until they pass from sight beyond the curve of the drive. When I turn around, Mrs Pearse is crying. She held back her tears while her sons were here, but now she gives in. She takes a handkerchief from her bosom to wipe her eyes.

Margaret is not crying – not quite – but her eyes look very red and her lower lip is quivering.

Until now this has all been a huge adventure. But if the women are frightened, if they are actually grieving even before anything happens ... gooseflesh prickles up my arms.

'Come through, John Joe,' says Margaret, 'and we shall have some breakfast.'

I go to the kitchen with the women and keep them company while Mrs Pearse prepares a meal large enough for five people. I don't point out that two hungry mouths will be missing. She knows.

Over breakfast we three try to make conversation

but it falls flat. The women are so obviously upset that I don't want to leave them alone, so I stay at table longer than usual. At last Mrs Pearse asks me to help her clear the table and wash the dishes.

I wonder what's happening in Dublin?

Finally I am free to go up to the dormitory. The large, empty room is full of shadows. The neatly made beds are lined up like so many soldiers. For a moment I stop and listen to the echo of my footfalls on the bare floor. I find myself imagining the sound of marching feet in Dublin.

At St Enda's it's easy to imagine all the things that have been, and all those that will be.

It's hard to know what to take with me. I have no weapons. In the Fianna we've had plenty of target practice but not with live ammunition, and the weapons we use are locked away afterwards. I suspect they've gone with the Volunteers now. If I'm right, there will be no shooting anyway. The important thing is to make a huge showing, to have lots and lots of us to impress the British.

Once I get into the city shall I stay there all day, or shall I return to the Hermitage? I suppose it depends on what's happening. Perhaps I had best be prepared for a long stay.

Taking the blanket and pillow off my bed, I roll them

into a cylinder to strap to the back of my bicycle. Then I put on my overcoat. The day is bright but very cold, and might be colder by the time I return.

It does not take very long to cycle to Roger's house. No one answers my knock at the front door. When I wander around to the back garden I find Roger there, playing with his dog. It's a nice dog, a big shaggy brown fellow called Mumbles. Mumbles looks like an oversized floor mop and loves everyone. Although Roger is surprised to see me, the dog rushes up to me and nearly knocks me down with his greeting.

I wish I had a dog. It's never been allowed.

'Where's the rest of your family, Roger?'

'They went to call on my grandmother who lives in Monkstown. They'll be back later. I suppose I should have gone with them but I hate visiting old people, all they ever talk about is the past.'

'So what are you going to do today?'

'I don't know.'

'Did you hear about the cancellation of the Rising?'

He nods glumly. 'My father read about it in the paper. It wasn't called a rising, though. Just "military manoeuvres".'

'Suppose I told you that those manoeuvres will take place after all. Today.'

Roger is staring at me. 'Are you sure?'

'Sure as eggs. Mr Pearse and Willie went into Dublin right after Mass. I'm on my way in myself and I thought you might like to come along.'

Roger's face is suddenly flushed. 'Are the Fianna called out after all, then?'

'Not us, just the older boys. But there's nothing to stop us from going in if we want to. You want to see it, don't you?'

Roger gives a yelp of joy. 'Wait right here, I'll fetch some provisions!'

He runs into his house and soon returns with coat pockets bulging. This time I must remember to ask for a share before he eats everything himself.

Roger orders Mumbles to 'Stay and guard the house'. Then we set off. We have not gone very far before Roger asks, 'Does the Ardmháistir know you're coming, John Joe?'

'He does not.'

'What will he say if we suddenly appear, when we've had orders to stay out of it?'

'He's going to be in the GPO setting up Headquarters. As long as we don't go there, he won't even see us.'

'Where are we going to be, then?'

'I've been thinking about that, Roger. Since it's a bank holiday the shops on Sackville Street will be closed, but the hotels should be open. We can probably see everything that happens from the Metropole or the Imperial.'

'Won't that be dangerous? What if the British decide to attack? Like with cannons or …'

'Rubbish. They aren't going to fire any cannons in Dublin. James Connolly says because the British are capitalists they will never attack property.'

'How do you know what Mr Connolly says?'

'Willie told me.' I cannot resist boasting, 'He tells me everything.' It's a lie, but only a little one. I'll tell it in Confession and be forgiven. I'm glad I'm a Catholic. What can Roger do if he tells lies?

Actually Willie is not one of the leaders, not a member of the inner circle of IRB men. It is hard to imagine anyone as shy and gentle as Willie Pearse as a revolutionary. I suspect he's a Volunteer only because he adores his older brother and wants to do whatever Padraic Pearse does.

We all feel like that.

As we pedal into the city, at first everything seems peaceful. Dubliners are enjoying their holiday. A stylishly dressed couple stroll together with linked arms; a boy not much younger than we are is rolling a hoop down the road; two little girls are playing with dolls on their front stoop.

When we turn into Harcourt Street I notice several people on the footpath, staring in the direction of St Stephen's Green. Just outside Harcourt Street Station a large crowd has gathered. They are talking excitedly to one another with quite a bit of arm waving.

'What's happening?' Roger calls to a stout man in a bowler hat.

Bowler Hat says, 'You'd best go home, lads. There's been some rifle fire.'

We immediately pull over to the kerb. 'Where, when?'

'It began this morning,' he tells us. 'At first we thought it was military practice, or maybe another march of the Volunteers letting off a few volleys out of high spirits, but ...'

A woman in a big hat with a feather on it interrupts. 'Rebels are attempting to seize the city!'

'What?' I try to look surprised.

'It's true,' says an elderly gentleman with the erect bearing of a soldier. 'A motley crew of insurgents gathered around eleven o'clock at Liberty Hall and marched to the General Post Office, which they have wantonly occupied. Others have attacked Dublin Castle and still another band is dug in at Stephen's Green. I don't know what this country's coming to. We can't have this sort of thing. We simply cannot allow it!'

Roger and I exchange glances.

I silently mouth 'The Metropole', and he nods.

We make those bicycles almost fly!

In the next block there are barricades. Motor cars have been driven into the middle of the street and abandoned to block traffic. We get around them easily enough on our bicycles, though.

Civilians crowd the footpaths in Westmoreland Street and everything looks normal, except for the soldiers. There are too many soldiers in the street, and even more policemen, milling about as if uncertain what to do. That means the element of surprise has been in our favour. Mr Pearse will be pleased.

When we reach the quays we see deserted tram cars with no one in them, not even the conductor.

At the foot of Sackville Street the O'Connell Bridge is guarded by some of the older Fianna boys, carrying rifles. One of the lads recognises us. 'Mr Pearse is expecting me!' I shout at him without slowing down. 'We have an urgent message from St Enda's!'

They let us pass.

From Kelly's Corner northwards everything looks different. The pubs appear to be open and a lot of people are wandering up and down the street, but there are also barricades made of overturned carts and rubbish and bits of furniture from nearby tenements.

Barbed wire has been strung in some places. Armed Volunteers are much in evidence now; also men in Citizen Army uniforms. Several women hurry up the street carrying ammunition boxes.

I started to say this is no place for women, but I realise that's not true. This is everyone's fight. If Marcella were here she would carry ammunition boxes, and I would be proud of her for doing it. I don't think about girls in the same way I once did. Knowing Madame has ...

'Look up!' cries Roger, pointing.

The windows in the top stories of several buildings have been broken out. Hidden snipers sweep the barrels of their rifles up and down the street.

The silver-haired doorman at the Metropole is attired in a splendid uniform with gold braid on his chest, but he does not look the least bit military. He looks extremely anxious.

As we lean our bicycles against the wall he asks, 'Are you lads guests here?'

'Our father is,' I say without hesitation. 'He sent for us.'

'And right too,' says the doorman. 'You lads should be off the streets.' He holds open the heavy glass door and we hurry inside.

The lobby is painted in rich dark colours; it takes my

eyes a few moments to adjust from the brightness of the street outside. Then I see a clerk behind the desk looking at me.

Putting on my best smile, I walk over to him. 'Mam sent me to fetch my father. She's frightened and wants him to come home.'

'Is your father stopping with us?'

'He's visiting one of your guests. On the third floor,' I add. 'Can you direct me to the stairs?'

'Certainly, young man.' The clerk leans forward across the desk. 'Turn to your left and go straight along that passageway.'

Roger trots hastily after me. Once we're out of sight of the clerk he gives a low whistle. 'You're very clever, you are.'

From the street comes a sound like a rifle shot.

Roger and I bolt up the stairs.

I lead the way to the very top floor, where we walk along the hallway until we come to an open doorway. Peering in, I see that the room is unoccupied. The bed is neatly made and the curtains are drawn. 'Come on, Roger,' I hiss as I dart inside.

We close the door behind us and stand breathing hard.

'Now what?' says Roger.

I don't know. This is as far as my imagination has

brought us. 'Open the curtains and see if you can see the street. I'm turned around, I don't know which way this room faces.'

When Roger looks out the window he gives a little gasp. 'There are four ... no, five ... policemen down there.'

'Are they coming in?'

'I don't think so, they're just talking to each other. Now they're walking away ... no they aren't. Two of them are coming back. It looks like they've been posted outside the lobby.'

If they have, we had best stay here until they leave. I wish I had thought things through better.

Roger sits down on a chair beside a small table and begins unloading his pockets. 'We might as well eat while we wait,' he says philosophically.

I have never been in a hotel room before. It is clean and very nice, but the air smells stale. I don't want to open a window for fear of drawing attention to ourselves. There is nothing here to entertain two boys who came to join a revolution. The afternoon drags by. The atmosphere in the room is growing stuffy. We hear the rattle of gunfire in the distance; then it seems to come closer. There is a lot of unidentified noise out in the street. I'm reluctant to try to leave the hotel, though. The policemen are still outside. They might ask questions I cannot answer.

When someone knocks on the door, I jump. 'Who is it?'

'The chambermaid, sir. Do you want your bed turned down before we leave?'

Do hotel staff leave at night? I don't know. I've never stayed in a hotel.

'We can do it ourselves,' I call out. When we hear her footsteps walking away, I turn the key in the door. 'I guess we're here for the night, Roger. It's dusk outside now; we could never ride all the way home in the dark.'

'Will they charge us for the room, John Joe?'

I had not thought about that. 'Not if they don't know we're here.'

'But the chambermaid knows.'

This is growing complicated. I want to leave but I'm not sure how to go about it. And besides, I'm getting sleepy.

'Maybe the best thing is just to go to bed,' I tell Roger. 'We're safe enough here, and warm. In the morning we'll find a way to sneak out.'

He must be sleepy too, because he does not argue. We crawl into the one big bed and snuggle under the covers.

And that's the last thing I remember.

CHAPTER SEVENTEEN

TUESDAY, EASTER WEEK 1916

When I wake up, at first I don't know where I am. Everything looks strange. Roger is lying beside me, snoring like rocks rattling in a tin bucket. I reach over and shake his shoulder. 'Stop making that noise.'

'Hunh? What?' He sits up and looks blearily around. 'Where are we?'

By now I know where we are. I recall everything very clearly, but it is not very comforting. 'We're on the top floor of the Metropole Hotel but we have to get out of here. Don't you remember what happened yesterday? The Rising started and we're right in the middle of it.'

'Oh good,' says Roger, absolutely deadpan. 'Is our side winning?' He can be funny when one least expects it. I can never tell if he does it deliberately or he's just being Roger.

Cautiously opening the door of our room, I peer out. There is no one in the hallway. The hotel is eerily quiet.

At my shoulder, Roger asks, 'Is there not a kitchen here?'

'I'm sure there is.'

'Then why don't we smell food cooking?'

We find a toilet and wash-hand basin at the end of the passage and make ourselves as tidy as possible. There is not much we can about our clothes, which are badly rumpled. We should have taken them off before we went to bed but we were too sleepy then, and it's too late now.

When we are as ready as we're going to be, I lead the way down the stairs to the ground floor. We don't meet anyone on the stairs. Is the hotel deserted? Did something terrible happen last night while we were asleep?

I'm relieved to see there is a desk clerk on duty, though not the same one who was here yesterday.

Otherwise the lobby is empty. The clerk is making notes in a ledger. When he sees us he pushes his spectacles up onto the top of his bald head.

'Where did you boys come from?'

'Our room,' I reply with a careless upward wave. At the same time I glance toward the glass doors. No policemen.

'Are your parents still up there?' asks the clerk.

'They've already gone out.'

'To have breakfast,' Roger interjects. 'We're just about to join them.' He hurries across the lobby and pushes a door open, then turns back toward me. 'Come look at this, John Joe! The street's full of paper!'

I join him to stare in amazement. From the O'Connell Monument to the Pillar, shop windows are smashed and litter lies everywhere. There are no policemen or British soldiers to be seen, only our own Volunteers. They look like real soldiers themselves now as they run, bent over, from one position to another.

The air stinks of bitter smoke.

There is the sound of a rifle shot. A chip of stone from the façade of the hotel flies past my face.

'Janey Mack!' Roger almost knocks me down as he tumbles back into the lobby.

The desk clerk runs over to us. 'You boys can't go out there now, it's not safe. I don't know where your parents are but if they left you here, this is where you should be. They'll come and find you when they can.'

I can hear the sound of heavy firing coming from the quays.

'This is real,' Roger says breathlessly. I don't think he's trying to be funny.

'Very real,' agrees the clerk. 'The Sinn Féiners are staging a rebellion.'

I start to tell him it's not the 'Sinn Féiners', but he's in no mood to listen. 'They must be crazy to try something like this,' he says angrily. 'I pray the authorities put a stop to them before it goes any further. It's emptying out the hotel.'

I draw myself up to my full height and glare at him. 'Don't you want Ireland to be free?'

'Free? Free of what?'

'Of Britain, of course! Of foreign domination!'

'You don't know what you're talking about, son. Everything was perfectly fine until yesterday.'

Roger retorts, 'It may have been fine for you. You have a job and enough food to put in your belly. But there are thousands of people in Dublin who go to bed hungry every night. The authorities don't care. It's all right with them as long as plenty of Irish soldiers fight King George's war, and plenty of Irish produce is shipped to English tables.'

I turn to stare at my friend. All those hours in the classroom, when he was gazing out the window and I thought he was daydreaming, he must have been listening after all. Some time between the death of his brother and yesterday morning, Roger has turned into a rebel.

The gunfire is almost continuous now. While I am trying to decide what to do next, a man rushes into the lobby. 'The looters are throwing every sort of merchandise out the windows of Lawrence's! There's a dead horse at the top of the street and a bonfire between Nelson's Pillar and the Parnell Monument. I've never seen anything like it.'

To his credit, the desk clerk keeps his wits about him. 'Do you wish to check out, Mr Preston?'

'Where would I go? I came to Dublin on business and there's no business to be done today. No, give me my room key and I'll stay here for now. At least I'll be in a good position to know what's happening. But I'm going to have my bags packed. I warn you,' he shakes a finger at the desk clerk as if it's all his fault, 'I am going to have my bags packed!'

He disappears up the stairs.

So the hotel is not empty after all. Maybe this is the best place for us to be, too. 'We'll wait for our parents upstairs,' I tell the clerk. Seizing Roger's hand, I tug him after me.

We don't return to the top storey, though. On the first floor we find an empty room – obviously just vacated, the bed is still unmade – and settle in. The windows give a good view of the street. And we're that bit closer to the action.

Thus we see the first squad of Volunteers arrive to take over the Metropole. They enter the lobby without firing a shot. A few minutes later two of them escort our desk clerk out the door. One walks with him all the way to the Bridge to see that he gets across safely.

'Now no-one knows where we are,' says Roger. 'Should we not go down to the lobby and tell the Volunteers we're here?'

'And have them turn us over to the Ardmháistir? I think not. He would insist on sending us away.'

We hear a lot of noise below as the ground floor windows are smashed and barricaded. A few more guests – including the excitable business man – leave, again politely escorted by Volunteers. Then the hotel falls quiet.

It is not quiet outside. Gunfire, shouting, the wail of an ambulance … and somewhere off in the distance a more ominous sound, like gunfire magnified many times.

'Is that artillery, John Joe?'

'It must be.'

'Do you suppose our reinforcements have arrived yet?'

'I don't see any more Volunteers out there than we saw yesterday.'

'But they will come, won't they?'

'I'm sure they will, Roger.'

There is a lone newsboy across the street with a bundle of papers under his arm. I wonder if I dare run across and buy one?

A little scouting locates a back stair that leads to a door in the alleyway. Leaving Roger to guard the door and be sure to open it for me when I return, I wait until there is a lull in the commotion in the street, then dart across and buy a newspaper. I hold it so tightly in my sweating hand that the newsprint smears onto my fingers.

Back in our room we eagerly spread the paper out on the unmade bed. Then we discover it is Monday's edition. 'No new news,' Roger says regretfully.

Yesterday's news is bad enough.

Thanks to Eoin MacNeill's countermand, it appears that the Volunteers down the country believed the Rising was cancelled. So they are not on their way. Even if they did set out now, it would be too late. The British are already ordering large numbers of troops into Ireland to quell 'the insurgency'.

It will be just our small band against the might of the Empire.

By leaving our windows open in spite of the cold, throughout a long day we learn more bits and snatches of information as the men below in the street call out to one another.

Yesterday afternoon – and oh, I wish I'd been there to hear it! – Padraic Pearse read out the Proclamation of the Irish Republic in front of the General Post Office. The GPO is now officially the General Headquarters of the Provisional Government of the Irish Republic.

Both Mr Pearse and James Connolly, who is Commandant-General of the Dublin Division, are there, together with a mixed force of Volunteers and Citizen Army. Joe Plunkett is Chief-of-Staff. Some of the older Fianna are in General Headquarters too, where the women of Cumann na mBan are providing a commissary.

The First Battalion of Irish Volunteers, under the command of Edward Daly, Tom Clarke's brother-in-law, has occupied the Four Courts. When we learn that the Second Battalion under Thomas MacDonagh is in Jacob's Biscuit Factory, Roger gives a sigh of envy.

'War,' I remind him, 'is about more than getting your hands on an unlimited supply of sweet biscuits.'

At Boland's Mills and Bakery, the Third Battalion is commanded by Éamon de Valera. Éamonn Ceannt and the Fourth Battalion have taken over the South Dublin Union.

Battles are raging everywhere.

'Is there a chance we can win?' Roger asks me. He means we the Irish, not we the British. All of us Irish together.

I cannot give him an answer, I simply don't know enough.

If Roger were not with me I would go to the GPO. That's where I want to be. The Ardmháistir might be angry with me, but he would understand. I feel responsible for Roger, however. He would be no good in a real fight, he would just get himself hurt. He's safe enough here for the time being, so I had best stay here with him.

From conversation in the street below we discover that an attempt by the Citizen Army to seize Dublin Castle yesterday was not successful. But Countess Markievicz is second-in-command at Stephen's Green. On our way into the city we almost came right past her. If I had known, that's where we would be now.

I'll bet she would let us fight.

We are getting very hungry, so we go on another scouting expedition. The Volunteers are on the ground floor but no one is in the cellar, where the larder is. Roger and I manage to sneak down without being seen. We soon hurry back to our room with bread and cheese and cold meat and tinned fruit. Roger wants to bring a basket of eggs until I remind him we have no way to cook them.

We have left a note in the larder, listing the supplies we've taken and promising to make it good when the revolution is over. I keep a similar list to be sure the debt is paid in full.

As we eat we can hear machine-gun fire; it seems to be coming from the south quays. I never heard it before but the sound is unmistakeable. Rat-a-tat-tat-tat-tat-tat. Vicious.

The food sits like a stone in my stomach. Even Roger doesn't eat very much. He tears his bread into pieces and rolls it into little pellets, like ammunition.

In mid-afternoon, someone in the street announces in a loud voice that martial law has been declared in Dublin.

Eventually we decide we might as well go to bed. There's nothing else to do anyway, and the light is beginning to fade. After making a last trip to look out the window into the street, I throw back the covers and stretch out with my arms folded behind my head.

There are cracks in the plaster on the ceiling. I try to make them form a map of the world, but they are not in the right places.

Just as I am dozing off, there is a scratching at the door.

'Roger. Sssst, Roger, do you hear that?'

'I do hear it. What do you think it is?'

'Rats, maybe.'

'In the Metropole? I doubt that! My parents have stayed in the Metropole Hotel.' It is Roger, not me, who gets out of bed and pads across to the door. 'Who's there?'

'Are you with the Fianna?' asks a high-pitched voice.

'Who wants to know?'

'Conor and Francis and Gerry. We're Fianna too.'

Roger flings open the door. There stand three little boys, silhouetted against the gaslight in the hallway.

By now I'm on my feet. 'How did you find us?'

'Can we come in?'

'Hurry before someone sees you!'

'No-one will see us, they're asleep downstairs. Even the sentry at the door. We tiptoed right past him.'

We know these boys, we've all drilled together. The speaker, whose name is Conor, is perhaps a year younger than I am and is wearing long trousers. The other two are still in short pants.

I fold my arms on my chest and try to sound stern. 'You have no business being here, you'll have to go home.'

The littlest boy lets out a wail. 'Tell him, Conor! Tell him we can't go home!'

Conor says, 'When we heard what was happening yesterday we decided to come and see for ourselves. So we walked into town. We got all the way to the bottom of Sackville Street before anyone even spoke to us. Then things got very scary. We hid under some debris for a while. When we finally crawled out I looked up and saw you in the window, John Joe. We want to join the fighting too.'

'You can't join the fighting,' I try to tell them. 'Roger and I aren't fighting, we're just here. As observers,' I add, to make it sound official.

'Well, we can't go back. There are lots of British soldiers between us and home.'

'Surely they would let three children pass through their lines unharmed.'

Conor looks as if he might cry. 'You don't understand. We don't want to pass through their lines. We want to stay here and fight!'

What are we going to do with them?

CHAPTER EIGHTEEN

WEDNESDAY, EASTER WEEK 1916

Now that our little band has expanded, I decide we should go back to the top floor. It might be safer there. However the five of us spend an uncomfortable night. I insist we stay together in the same room, which means there is only the one bed. We can all lie across it width-wise, but it is almost impossible for anyone to turn over. Besides, my feet hang over the edge. Finally I make pallets out of the bedclothes and put them on the floor for the younger boys. Roger and I sleep on the bed with our overcoats for cover.

The people in the GPO must be a lot more

uncomfortable than we are. The gunfire is continuing off and on, even at night.

By morning Roger is not the only one complaining about being hungry. Leaving Conor in charge, he and I return to the larder. The Volunteers must have discovered it; there is hardly any food left. I insist we save what there is for the little boys. Roger grumbles but agrees. It's obvious, though, that we cannot stay here for much longer without anything to eat.

I decide on a bold tactic. Beyond the service entrance of the hotel is the alley where deliveries are made – when anyone is making deliveries. The alley leads me into a narrow street that gives on to another narrow street, and that to yet another. I find a number of small shops – all closed and shuttered – and, at last, a pub that's still open.

Yet not far a way there is the constant sound of gunfire.

Now is not the time to be manly. I need to look like a starving child. Fortunately, I've studied acting at St Enda's; I know how to convince an audience. First you have to believe it yourself.

I recall the pains that gnawed my belly when my father shut me in my room all day and all night without anything to eat. When you've been really hungry you can never forget it.

Then I scoop up a handful of muck from the gutter and smear it across my face. Turning up my coat collar, I bend my knees to make myself shorter, and walk timidly into the bar.

The barman has a face like a boiled pudding. 'Wot's yer pleasure, guv'nor?'

He's mocking me but I don't care. 'Please, sir, my little brothers and sisters are hungry. Our parents went out yesterday and haven't come back. I don't know what's happened to them. I'm scared.'

His expression softens. 'They'll be all right, lad. You run on home and wait for them.'

'But what will we eat?'

Fifteen minutes later I'm back at the Metropole with a big jar of pickled eggs and some brown bread and sugar and lemons and cold bacon and a packet of tea. The barman even gave me an almost-sharp knife to cut the bread. How we will brew the tea I do not know.

The little boys fall on the food like ravening wolves. Roger, who is more resourceful than I realised, searches the empty bedrooms on this floor until he finds five drinking glasses. He fills the glasses with hot water from the tap in the basin. We dump in the tea and wait until the brew turns a sort of pale brown. Then we squeeze some lemons into it and add a lot of sugar.

It's the best tea I ever tasted.

After we finish eating, I unfold a sheet of paper from my coat pocket and spread it out on the bed. 'Look at this, lads. These are posted on walls all around here, so I took one down for us.'

The boys gather around a creased copy of the Proclamation of the Irish Republic. The type is black and rather smudged. Roger begins to read aloud:

'Irishmen and Irishwomen: In the name of God and of the dead generations from which she receives her old tradition of nationhood, Ireland, through us, summons her children to her flag and strikes for her freedom.

'Having organised and trained her manhood through her secret revolutionary organisation, the Irish Republican Brotherhood,' – I know about them! – 'and through her open military organisations, the Irish Volunteers and the Irish Citizen Army …'

In my mind's eye I can see Padraic Pearse standing in front of the GPO. What courage it must have taken to read these words out loud in a land that has been occupied by a foreign power for over seven hundred years!

'We declare the right of the people of Ireland to the ownership of Ireland.'

The ownership of Ireland! I have a lump in my throat. *Our own land!*

'We hereby proclaim the Irish Republic as a Sovereign

Independent State ... We pledge our lives and the lives of our comrades-in-arms to the cause of its freedom, of its welfare, and of its exaltation among the nations ... The Republic guarantees civil and religious liberty, equal rights and equal opportunities to all its citizens, and declares its resolve to pursue the happiness and prosperity of the whole nation and of all its parts, cherishing all the children of the nation equally ...'

There are seven signatures at the bottom. Thomas J. Clarke, Seán MacDiarmada, P. H. Pearse, James Connolly, Thomas MacDonagh, Eamonn Ceannt, and Joseph Plunkett.

The words of the Proclamation are still ringing in my ears when we hear a terrible booming explosion. We all run to the windows. From the direction of the river an immense cloud of dust is billowing into the sky.

One of the Fianna guarding the bridge comes running up Sackville Street, waving his arms and shouting. 'The British have a gunboat on the Liffey! They've fired on Liberty Hall!'

Within minutes a terrific bombardment is striking the area around Butt Bridge and the Customs House. The noise is deafening. We can see the occasional leap of flames above the rooftops. 'They must be firing incendiary shells,' Roger remarks. 'I've read about those, they're being used in Europe.'

Mr Connolly was wrong about British capitalists. They *will* destroy property – so long as it's Irish.

Our troops are firing back with everything they have. We don't have to go looking for the war, it's all around us. Something smashes against the side of the Metropole and the entire hotel shudders. Plaster flakes fall from the ceiling and pepper my shoulders like dandruff. The little boy called Francis shouts, 'It's snowing indoors!'

Another tremendous explosion, very near, sounds even worse. 'What was that?' I shout down to the nearest man in the street.

'The GPO. I think something hit the top storey.' He starts to run in that direction.

Will the Commander-in-Chief order an evacuation? I do not think so. I know Mr Pearse. He will not run.

How I wish there was something we could do to be useful. But all around is total confusion. If we go out into the street we have no orders and no weapons, we would just be in the way.

Funnily enough, I'm not afraid of being hurt. I suppose I should be, but I'm not. Something deep inside me has become very calm and quiet, like Mr Pearse.

'What shall we do, sir?' Gerry, the smallest of the boys, asks me. Me. Sir!

'We are going to stay here for now and keep a sharp lookout. I don't know what will happen next but we must be ready for anything.'

'We are sir,' the little lad says cheerfully.

I reach out and tousle his hair.

The shelling goes on and on. At first every explosion makes us flinch violently, but after a while one almost gets used to the noise. Otherwise one would soon be exhausted. Much of the city, at least that part which we can see from here, is being laid to waste. I wonder when it will be our turn.

We hear a commotion in the passageway, then a thunderous knock at the door. 'Who's in there?'

We freeze.

'In the name of the Republic!' another voice cries. 'Is anyone in there?'

I run to the door and throw it open.

Four men wearing civilian clothes and Volunteer badges stare back at me. It is hard to say who is more surprised, me or them. 'What are you lot doing up here?' one asks, indicating the other boys in the room.

'We're Fianna, sir. We came to see the fighting.'

He cannot help grinning. 'Seen enough yet, have you?'

'We've seen a bit but we don't know what's happening.'

'The British are closing in on us, that's what's happening. We've had to evacuate some of our wounded, but we're still holding Headquarters.'

'Is the Ard … is the Commander-in-Chief all right?' I want to know.

'Pearse is amazing, as cool as well water. I don't think he's slept at all since Monday. He spends his time either going around and encouraging the troops, or writing a 'newspaper' as he calls it, trying to keep up our spirits by telling us how well everything's going.'

Roger asks, 'Is everything going well?'

'Hardly. We're done for, though no-one's willing to admit it. We'll hold out for as long as we can, though. Let'em know they've been in a scrap. Me and my men have been assigned to take over this floor of the hotel as a sniper post. We did not know anyone was still up here, not until we heard voices in this room. Mind if we join you?'

'We would be honoured, sir,' says Conor.

The Volunteers take up positions, two in each of our two windows. I am almost certain that the rifles they carry were part of the Howth cargo. The men watch the street below with frightening intensity, and we watch them. Every now and then one sights along his rifle and squeezes off a shot. I notice that they are careful with their ammunition.

'Have your men had anything to eat today?' I ask their leader. His name, I have learned, is Captain Fitzsimons. 'We have some pickled eggs. And we can make tea for you.'

The captain rewards my offer with a weary smile. 'Just when I thought we were all out of miracles.'

CHAPTER NINETEEN

THURSDAY, EASTER WEEK 1916

None of us slept well last night.

At precisely ten o'clock in the morning the British begin bombarding Lower Sackville Street. One building after another goes on fire. Kelly's Gun Shop, on the corner by the bridge, is abandoned, and the men who were holding that position retreat to the GPO. Captain Fitzsimons leans out a window to shout to them, 'Good job lads, keep the heart up!'

I'm glad we have the snipers with us, because from time to time a messenger brings them news. It's the job I should have had, being a messenger.

We learn that the British gunboat *Helga* is not doing all of the damage to Dublin. Field guns are being fired from Trinity College as well, adding to the bombardment and destruction. Students of the Officers' Training Corps are manning the university as a temporary garrison until the British military take over.

Last night there was a huge battle at the Mount Street Bridge. For five hours a mere handful of Volunteers in Clanwilliam House held out against a whole British column.

Although most of the Citizen Army have been forced to evacuate their outposts, about a hundred are still in the Royal College of Surgeons across from St Stephen's Green. Among them is Constance Markievicz.

I am confident that Madame, like Mr Pearse, will fight to the last.

From the sounds of battle we can tell that the British army is drawing closer and closer. They are tightening a noose around all our necks. Yet there is no talk of trying to escape. Even little Gerry seems quite unafraid.

Just a few minutes ago Captain Fitzsimons gave an exclamation of surprise. 'Come over here John Joe,' he says beckoning me to his window. 'Look down there. What do you see?'

I can hardly believe my eyes. Seven more young boys are cautiously making their way up Sackville

Street, dodging from building to building while gunfire echoes all around them. 'Do you know any of that lot?' the captain asks me.

'All of them. They're Fianna from St Enda's.'

'Stay here,' he says sternly. We hear him running down the passage. Shortly afterward he appears in the street. He uses an ear-splitting whistle to get the boys' attention. When they look in his direction he gives a commanding wave. After a moment's hesitation, they trot over to him and he ushers them into the hotel.

Captain Fitzsimons herds his flock into our room and closes the door firmly behind them. He looks as if he does not know whether to laugh or cry. I can under-stand his feelings.

'You lads could have been killed,' the captain says.

'We know that, sir. But we weren't.'

'Why have you done such a foolish, foolish thing?'

The newcomers look at one another, and then at me. I guess it is because I am the tallest member of the Fianna in the room. 'We belong here,' one boy says simply.

Mid-morning we have a visitor. James Connolly, a stocky, sturdy man in Citizen Army uniform and leather leggings, is making the rounds of the sniper positions. When he enters the room on the top floor – which is rather crowded by this time – he opens his eyes very wide indeed. 'Captain,' he asks Fitzsimons, 'what is the meaning of this?'

'You had best ask them, sir.'

'I certainly shall,' Connolly says gruffly. 'Just what are you lads playing at?'

'We're auxiliaries, sir,' I reply.

'Nonsense.'

'But we are. We're members of the Fianna.'

'Nonsense,' Connolly says again. 'You're only children. Don't you know there's a war going on?'

I decide to brazen it out. 'Boys our age have fought in wars since the beginning of history. Mr Pearse believes we are of strategic importance,' I add recklessly.

James Connolly laughs, a great booming laugh. 'Does he now? I'll tell you what. You stay here while I go ask him what he wants done with you. Don't go outside at all, do you understand? That's an order!'

'Yes sir.'

'And keep your heads below the window sills!' he adds as he strides away.

The gunfire is coming closer and closer. The crash of falling bricks and mortar from the areas around Sackville Street is almost constant. The centre of Dublin is being torn apart by British artillery. The captain and his men stand well back from the windows now, though they have their rifles at the ready.

After fifteen or twenty minutes Connolly returns. 'I suppose you lads will have to stay,' he tells us. 'Pearse agreed with me that it would be too dangerous to try to send you home.' Connolly smiles. 'Actually, what he said was, 'I suggest you provide them with weapons. They may have to defend not only their ideals but themselves.' So I've brought you three old pistols, all we could spare. Do you boys know how to shoot them? If not, I'm sure Captain Fitzsimons can show you.'

The pistols are given to Roger, Conor, and myself, together with a very few rounds of ammunition. The Volunteers take time to make sure we know how to use the weapons, then return to their posts.

The British are almost upon us now. Machine-gun fire constantly rakes the nearby streets.

A messenger arrives from Headquarters with the news that General Sir John Maxwell is on his way from England to take command of the British forces. Maxwell has a fearsome reputation. He is reported to have said he has no intention of sparing Dublin. He will not hesitate to destroy any buildings that may harbour what he calls 'rebels'.

Us. The insurgents. The Irish who want their country back.

In the afternoon we receive bad news indeed. James Connolly has been shot twice in the leg. He was taken to Headquarters, where the women are nursing the wounded. Although his injuries are very serious he refuses to stay quiet, but insists on being wheeled about on his bed so he can supervise the defence of the GPO.

Stepping up beside the Volunteers, we boys aim our pistols down into the street. The rebels in the Metropole Hotel want to shoot the man who shot Connolly.

We can hardly tell day from night anymore, the air is so filled with smoke and dust. I have lost all sense of time. We are just here. The noise and the destruction are everywhere. I cannot remember when things were any different.

This must be what hell is like.

And it goes on and on.

There is no light in the room except for the lurid glow from the fires burning in the ruins of buildings.

Finally Captain Fitzsimons orders his men to lie down for a while and try to get some sleep. We boys do the same. The room is very cold and we do not have enough blankets and coats to keep us warm, but it hardly matters. We would shiver anyway. From excitement or fear or tension. They all feel the same now.

You would not think anyone could sleep under such circumstances, but I am deep in a blurry dream about

Emmet's Fort and Roger's dog when voices over my head wake me up again.

The messenger who has visited us before is saying, 'There are twelve thousand British troops in Dublin now, and the centre of the city is cordoned off.'

Captain Fitzsimons asks, 'What of the other garrisons?'

'Since early this afternoon there has been no word from Daly at the Four Courts. MacDonagh and de Valera are holding firm so far, but Ceannt is taking heavy fire at the South Dublin Union. Cathal Brugha, his second-in-command, has been severely wounded.'

'And James Connolly? How is he now?'

'It does not look good for him, sir. His wounds are dreadfully inflamed and causing him a lot of pain.'

The captain says, 'Thank you for coming to tell us. Please continue to keep us informed about the situation.'

'I don't know how much longer that will be possible, sir. A lot of our messengers have been trapped elsewhere, and we're very short-handed at Headquarters. We don't even have enough stretcher-bearers left.'

I am totally and completely awake.

Scrambling to my feet, I tell Captain Fitzsimons, 'I'm big enough to be a stretcher-bearer. May I go to Headquarters?'

'What about me?' wails Roger. 'Don't leave me, John Joe!'

'Can you get these two boys safely back there with you?' the captain asks the messenger.

'I can try, sir.'

'Very well, you may take them.'

And then, so swiftly we don't have time to think, Roger and I are running down the hotel passageway behind the messenger from Headquarters. Running down the carpeted stairs which are gritty underfoot now, running across the lobby which is half-filled with debris, running out into the terrible street.

CHAPTER TWENTY

FRIDAY, EASTER WEEK 1916

I do not know what I expected, but the General Post Office is very changed. An Irish tricolour, blackened with smoke, droops from the flagpole that always held the Union Jack before. The flames of the burning city provide enough light to reveal the dreadful damage done by British artillery. I am almost surprised that anyone could still be alive inside.

But they are.

Roger and I follow the messenger under the portico and into the lobby on the ground floor. It is filled with men and rubble and sandbags and broken glass and splintered timber. The smell is appalling. A mixture of smoke and sweat and blood and …

'Over here,' calls the messenger. He leads us to Joe Plunkett, the Chief-of-Staff, who is half-sitting, half-lying on a pile of debris draped with one of his great capes.

'I've found two more stretcher-bearers, sir,'

Plunkett looks ghastly. His face is deathly pale and there is a bandage around his throat with blood seeping through. Roger asks, 'Are you wounded yourself, sir?'

Plunkett gestures toward his throat with an elegant, long-fingered hand laden with heavy rings. 'Don't concern yourself, this is not a wound. I had an operation recently, that's all.'

'He has tuberculosis of the throat,' I whisper to Roger. 'Willie told me he was in Switzerland taking treatment, but he came back for this.'

I cannot tell if Joe Plunkett hears me. I cannot even tell if Roger hears me, for at that moment there is a dreadful crash overhead and ceiling debris cascades down upon us.

Why don't they stop! It's night-time, so why don't they *stop*?!

But it is not night-time. It is Friday morning. A pale, sickly light is beginning to filter into the ruin that is the

Headquarters of the Provisional Irish Republic.

The devoted women and girls who have kept the defenders fed and bandaged look as exhausted as the men, but they provide us with some tea and soup. It is the first hot food we have had in a long time. While Roger is still devouring his I wander around the lobby.

When curiosity prompts me to peer behind a hospital screen, I find James Connolly lying on old iron bedstead and reading a book. The loss of blood has left him almost as pale as Joe Plunkett. When he sees me he raises himself onto one elbow. 'There's one of our snipers now!' he says cheerfully. 'How are you, boy?'

'I'm well, sir. How are you?'

'I would be a lot better if they were not keeping me out of the action! When you see Pearse tell him, will you?'

'Where is Mr Pearse, sir? I have not yet seen him.'

'He's in that little makeshift office of his, writing something or other.' Connolly sounds dismissive, as if every man should be busy shooting every moment.

When I return to Joe Plunkett for my assignment, he tells me, 'You have not come a minute too soon. There is more work to be done than able-bodied men to do it.'

There is no mention of my age now.

My first job is to carry ammunition to the Volunteers

guarding the windows and doors. They are firing spar-
ingly, trying to make every shot count. Their eyes are
red with lack of sleep.

Tucked into my waistband is the pistol James Connolly gave me. Could I actually shoot someone with it?
I don't know. I don't suppose anyone ever really
knows until the moment comes.

After a while I go to the basement to see if there is
any more ammunition. The two toilets down there, the
only ones in the building, are blocked up and overflowing. The smell is terrible.

Shortly after I return, empty-handed, to the lobby, Mr
Pearse emerges from a room at the back. He is carrying
a handwritten sheet which he puts up on what remains
of the post office bulletin board. It is a manifesto filled
with praise for the brave men and women who have
carried the fight this far. The only person he mentions
by name is Mr Connolly, whom he calls 'the guiding
brain of our resistance'.

He has written, 'If they do not win this fight, they will
at least have deserved to win it. But win it they will,
although they may win it in death. Already they have
won a great thing. They have redeemed Dublin from
many shames, and made her name splendid among the
names of cities.'

The document continues, 'I am satisfied that we have

saved Ireland's honour. I am satisfied that we should have accomplished more had our arrangements for a simultaneous rising of the whole country been allowed to go through on Easter Sunday. Of the fatal counter-manding order which prevented those plans from being carried out, I shall not speak further. Both Eoin MacNeill and we have acted in the best interests of Ireland.

'For my part, as to anything I have done in this, I am not afraid to face either the judgment of God or the judgment of posterity.'

'Signed P. H. Pearse, Commandant General, Commanding-in-Chief, the Army of the Irish Republic, and President of the Provisional Government'.

I wish he had added 'Ardmháistir, Scoil Eanna'.

Mr Pearse summons all the women in the building and orders them to leave. A few nurses refuse, but most of the others reluctantly accept. He shakes hands with each of them as she departs.

If he is sending the women away that must mean it's almost all over. I want to speak to him, but cannot bring myself to ask the question. Instead I just catch his eye and nod.

Padraic Pearse beckons me closer. 'You were one of those boys at the Metropole Hotel,' he says. It is not a question.

'Yes sir. We wanted to be with you.'

'God bless you,' he says.

'And you sir.'

He moves off to speak to some of the other men. I watch their eyes following him.

Then there is a terrible crash right above our heads. Black smoke comes billowing down the main staircase and we can hear the crackle of flames somewhere above. The GPO is built of stone but fitted with timber, and timber will burn.

Is burning.

We are fighting on two fronts now; fighting back the increasingly determined British assault and fighting back the flames. Unfortunately we are out of water. Roger runs past me carrying a bucket full of sand from one of the sandbags.

By later afternoon our battle with the fire is lost. But it is the good clean flame and not the unthinking brutality of the enemy that will drive us from the GPO. Mr Pearse has sent a man called The O'Rahilly to scout the area for the best route of evacuation. He has not returned. So we must make a run for it.

As dusk settles over the savaged city, the stretcher bearers are summoned to carry out the wounded. To my great pride I am assigned to help carry Connolly. He insists on being the last to leave – except for Mr

Pearse, who goes back into the flames one last time to make certain everyone is out of the GPO.

Then we set out for Moore Lane.

No sooner do we leave the protection of the post office doorway than British snipers open up on us. I hear the bullets spanging against the walls. Joe Plunkett, coughing, and Seán MacDermott, limping, urge us on. A bullet narrowly misses the stretcher we are carrying. In another moment the hidden sniper will have James Connolly in his sights.

I hurl myself across on the stretcher, shielding Connolly's body with my own. I am so close to him I can see the pores on his nose.

I can see the pores on James Connolly's nose.

Then we are running again. Running frantically through a hail of bullets. Mr Pearse stumbles once, right into the line of fire, but quickly regains his feet. I hear other men gasp and groan, yet somehow we stumble on.

At the corner of Moore Street we come to a grocery shop. A grey-haired woman has the door open. 'This way!' she calls. 'Hurry!'

Crowded among stacks of tinned goods and bags of flour, we stand trying to catch our breath.

'Set me down easy, lads,' Connolly says. We set the stretcher on the floor. Only then do I realise that I never felt his weight while we were carrying him, I never even felt the cobbles under my feet. The last few minutes have been a dream.

Or perhaps I should say a nightmare.

And it is not over yet.

We soon hear soldiers in the street outside, searching for us. The grey-haired woman has bolted the door and shuttered the windows so the grocery appears to be closed. We are probably safe enough for now, but we cannot get out the way we came in.

Miraculously, Mr Pearse seems to have got what remains of Headquarters staff out alive, though Joe Plunkett is in very bad shape. He totters on his feet and looks as if he is about to faint. Aside from my own mother I never saw anyone who is dying, but I think he is.

We have several badly wounded men with us, including a British soldier whom George Plunkett, Joe's brother, found lying in the street and would not leave to die.

The kind woman who offered us sanctuary owns the grocery. She is a widow with several nearly-grown children, and they live over the shop. The family do what they can to make us comfortable. They put the most seriously wounded into their own beds, and empty the presses of blankets and quilts for the rest of us.

Joe Plunkett valiantly refuses the offer of a bed, as does Mr Pearse. James Connolly, who is growing feverish and does not seem to know where he is, makes no objections when we tuck him into the largest bed. His wounded leg is propped on pillows. Stores from the grocery provide the best meal any of us have enjoyed in a week, then Mr Pearse orders the Fianna boys and the wounded men to try to get some sleep.

The rest of the Volunteers set to work tunnelling into the rear of Hanlon's Fishmongers, which is next door, hoping to escape unseen through that route.

In the crowded apartment above the grocery the air is stifling. Yet compared to the last hours in the GPO it is as sweet as roses.

CHAPTER TWENTY-ONE

SATURDAY, EASTER WEEK 1916

I'm awfully sorry I got Roger into this, and awfully thankful Marcella isn't here. With every passing hour I grow more certain that we're all going to die. Yet Roger seems almost casual about it. The boy who complained about everything isn't complaining about anything. In a few short hours his face has changed into that of a man.

I wonder what my own face looks like.

The tunnelling was successful enough, but when the Volunteers broke through into Hanlon's they discovered British artillery just outside in Parnell Street, and there are machine gun nests everywhere.

We are trapped.

The widow offers to prepare breakfast for us, but no one – even Roger – feels like eating. James Connolly is conscious again but all he wants is water. He cannot get enough.

Mr Pearse spends a lot of his time looking out an upstairs window. The curtains hide him from the street, but they do not hide the street from him. Suddenly he gives a soft cry and buries his face in his hands.

When he looks up again, he says, in the saddest voice, 'I just saw them shoot down three civilians. A man, a woman, and a young girl were running up Moore Street carrying a white flag.

'And the British shot them.'

He sounds as if his heart is breaking.

Perhaps it is.

After several minutes he has a low-voiced conversation with the other leaders. There seems to be some sort of an argument, but Mr Pearse is adamant and at last they agree.

Mr Pearse announces, 'It has been decided. As Commander-in-Chief, I am going to surrender myself and submit to whatever punishment British justice demands – on the condition that the rest of you are granted amnesty and no more citizens are hurt.'

'No!' I cry out.

He merely shakes his head. 'Yes. They will destroy our city and everyone in it, and it must stop.'

'But they'll shoot you on sight,' someone else says.

Again Mr Pearse shakes his head. 'We must trust our opponents to act honourably, as we would if the situation were reversed.' He turns to one of the nurses who has come with us, Elisabeth Farrell. 'Miss Farrell, will you be so kind as to take my offer to the commander of the British forces? We will provide you with a white flag and...'

I do not hear the rest. In my head I am listening to earlier words. Hope for the best and dare the worst.

It is over. The surrender has been accepted, but the British insist it must be unconditional, or hostilities will resume within the hour. General Maxwell promises to show no mercy. I don't believe much the British say, but I believe that.

An automobile has taken Padraic Pearse to British headquarters to make the final arrangements. Then he will write out orders for the Volunteers to surrender. Unflinching and resolute, he went out holding his head high with pride. Not pride in himself, but pride in all the men and women who have stood with him.

James Connolly, fighting back his pain, is writing out a surrender order for the Citizen Army because they would not obey anyone else.

When all is concluded we march out of Moore Street and surrender our arms, including the pistol I never got to fire. I wish now that I had.

The Volunteers are marched away to spend the night on the grounds of the Rotunda. Tomorrow they will march on to prison to await their fate. The Fianna boys will not be sent to prison, though.

We are too young. Or so the British say.

But I know I shall never be young again. And for the rest of my life, part of me will still be in the General Post Office with Padraic Pearse and James Connolly and the bravest men ever born in Ireland.

CHAPTER TWENTY-TWO

AND THEN ...

Within a few short days, the seven signatories of the Proclamation were dead. Pearse and Clarke and MacDonagh, Plunkett and MacDermott and Connolly and Ceannt. And gentle Willie Pearse, who did not even sign the Proclamation. His only crime was loving his brother and wanting to be with him.

The British lined them up, a few each day, against a high stone wall in Kilmainham Jail. Then a rifle party shot them down.

Mr Pearse, Mr MacDonagh, and Mr Clarke were shot at dawn on the third of May. I don't dare let myself imagine that hurried, secret execution. The sun rose red with blood.

One of the witnesses to the executions said that all the men died well, but Thomas MacDonagh died like a prince. He would have liked that, I think. But oh, Mr Pearse! *Ardmháistir!* What did we lose when they shot you?

The following morning the cruel rifles cut down Willie Pearse and Joe Plunkett, who had been married to his sweetheart only the night before in the prison chapel.

The executions continued in spite of the fact that news of them was leaking out. Protests began mounting both in England and abroad. But no mercy was shown. Padraic Pearse had been named the first president of the newly-declared Irish Republic. By shooting him the British had assassinated a head of state. That didn't seem to bother them.

When America declared her independence they would have executed George Washington if they could have got their hands on him.

Relentlessly, the rest of the signatories and several captured military leaders, such as my friend Con Colbert, were killed. Seán MacDermott and James Connolly were the last to die.

Mr MacDermott defied them to the end; they say he made a brilliant speech at his court martial. Mr Connolly was shot while tied to a chair because he was too severely wounded to stand.

The Dublin newspapers condemned the leaders of the Rising as madmen. That's understandable, the British control those newspapers. Many Dubliners were furious about the Rising because it interrupted business and so many buildings had been destroyed. The wives of Irish men who were serving in the British army called the leaders of the Rising traitors. That's understandable too; those women were collecting their husband's army pay every week.

But after a few days, Dubliners began to acknowledge that it was British artillery which had destroyed their city, and not the rebels.

Those who actually had known Mr Pearse and Mr Connolly and the others began reminding people that the leaders of the Rising had been poets and teachers and trade unionists. They were without exception decent, high-principled men. Extraordinary men who had been willing to give their lives so that Ireland could be free.

Public opinion began to turn around.

Mrs Pearse closed St Enda's. Two black mourning wreaths were hung on the front gates. We boys had to ride out the storm at home. In my case, that meant Aunt Nell's house in Kildare because I refused to go back to my father. I shall never go back to him. I declare my independence, too.

Within weeks of the Rising, Ireland was a different place. A surprising number of people began saying they had been close personal friends of the leaders. And it was strange how many claimed to have fought in the GPO during Easter Week, 1916. If only a quarter of them had really been there, we would have defeated the enemy on the first day.

Now freedom – *saoirse,* in Irish – is on everyone's lips. The air sparkles with it. Men and women have a new spring in their step; they don't walk with their heads down any more. We're not willing to go back to being second class citizens in our native land. If we have to, we'll go to war to finish what was started on Easter Monday.

When Mr Pearse and Mr Connolly were murdered something bigger than them was born.

No men ever undertook a more desperate gamble. The odds against them were terrible, but they believed that the effort was more important than the outcome. It's up to us to prove their sacrifice was worth it. I mean to do my best.

The volleys of rifle fire at Kilmainham have slain our heroes but not their dream. They have given Ireland back her soul.

Author's Note

The boys and girls named in this novel are fictional, but are based on real young people who actually participated in the events described. The events themselves are part of Irish history. That includes the exploits of the smaller St Enda's boys who recklessly ignored Pearse's orders and sneaked into Dublin to take part in the Rising. Fortunately they all survived.

The adults in this book, with the exception of John Joe's family, Roger's family and Mr Preston in the Metropole Hotel, are part of Irish history too. The names of Pearse and Connolly and Markievicz and the others became famous throughout Ireland.

Following the Rising, British soldiers occupied the Hermitage. They searched the house from top to bottom for weapons; they even dug up the gardens, but found nothing.

Although the heartbroken Pearse family was in

mourning, in the autumn of 1916 Mrs Pearse re-opened St Enda's as a tribute to her sons. Thomas MacDonagh's brother Joseph served as Headmaster for a time. He was succeeded by Francis Burke, a former student. But without Padraic Pearse the school never regained its original excellence. His unique vision had been the heart and soul of St Enda's, which finally closed its doors for good in 1935.

After Ireland fought and won its War of Independence in 1921, both Mrs Pearse and her daughter Margaret served as senators in the Seanad. Upon their deaths St Enda's was bequeathed to the people of Ireland.

The writings of P. H. Pearse are still studied and admired by progressive educationalists around the world, though some of them are unaware of his connection with Ireland's struggle for freedom.

If you would like to know more about Padraic Pearse and the school he founded, I suggest you read:

Scéal Scoil Éanna, The Story of an Educational Adventure, published by the National Parks and Monument Service.

The Man Called Pearse, by Desmond Ryan, published by Maunsel and Co. Ltd.

Pádraic Pearse, by Hedley McCay, published by Mercier Press.

'St Enda's and Its Founder', from *The Complete Works of P. H. Pearse*, published by Phoenix Publishing Company.

A Significant Irish Educationalist, Séamas Ó Buachalla (editor), published by Mercier Press.

Best of all, visit Scoil Éanna itself, now the Pearse Museum in Rathfarnham, County Dublin. The Hermitage has changed very little since the Pearse brothers left it for the last time on Easter Monday, 1916.

Spend a little time sitting behind the desk in Padraic Pearse's office, or in the study hall with the stage on which his students produced the plays he wrote. Upstairs are the dormitories where boys like John Joe and Roger slept. If you listen carefully you may catch the echo of boyish voices.

Wander through the well-tended grounds and the woods beyond and try to imagine what a paradise this was for Irish boys who had never known such a school before. Experience the sense of peace, and of hope, that still linger at Scoil Éanna.

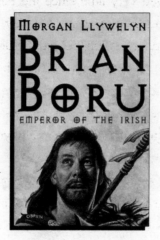

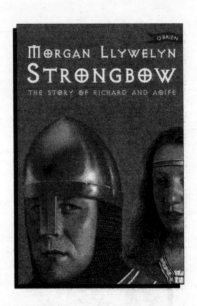

STRONGBOW
Winner Bisto Book of the Year Award
The dramatic story of the Norman conquest of Ireland in the twelfth century. Full of battles and warfare, but also a story of love between Aoife, a wilful Irish princess, and Strongbow, the greatest of the Norman knights to come to Ireland.

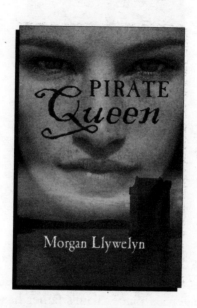

THE PIRATE QUEEN

A story of immense bravery and daring, as Granuaile takes on the great Norman lords, smuggles weapons and mercenaries for the Ulster Gaelic O'Donnell and O'Neill clans and finally goes to confront Elizabeth Tudor herself.

'This book ... is outstanding ... One can smell the sea and feel the slippery boards underfoot'
The Irish Post
'an amazing story of courage, determination and cunning'
The Irish Examiner

CAVE OF SECRETS

Pirates and crooked rulers make seventeenth-century Ireland a dangerous place. Tom's father has had savage losses in business and his whole world is under pressure. Tom starts mixing with smugglers in Roaringwater Bay and learns all about boats and smuggling – and secret treasure. And then Tom discovers the best-kept secret of all ...